CHRISTOPHER COE'S
I LOOK DIVINE

"I expect you pride yourself on being unaffected," my brother said to the woman.

"I do," the woman said.

"I don't," my brother said. "But I wonder all the time, who are people trying to fool, when they go through all their lives just acting like themselves."

He paused because he had come to a pause. After the pause, he said, "A little affection now and then is just a little generosity."

—From *I Look Divine* by Christopher Coe

"The two brothers remind us of Sebastian and Charles in *Brideshead Revisited*—conspiratorial, predatory, dispassionate yet intimate. And if Sebastian represents the British aristocracy strangling itself on its own ruling-class depravity, Nicholas represents a dying America, addicted to its image as a democracy even as it roams the world looking for 'conquests.'"

—SAN FRANCISCO CHRONICLE

I LOOK DIVINE

I LOOK DIVINE

Christopher Coe

VINTAGE CONTEMPORARIES
VINTAGE BOOKS
A DIVISION OF RANDOM HOUSE
NEW YORK

FIRST VINTAGE CONTEMPORARIES EDITION,
JANUARY 1989

Epigraph from Plutarch's *Life of Alcibiades*, .
Thomas North translation.

Library of Congress Cataloging-in-Publication Data
Coe, Christopher.
  I look divine.
  Reprint. Originally published: New York: Ticknor & Fields, 1987.
  I. Title.
PS3553.O34I2   1989   813'.54   88-40035
ISBN 0-394-75995-8 (pbk.)

Manufactured in the United States of America
10   9   8   7   6   5   4   3   2   1

For Hans Guggenheimer
For Majorie Edwards Brush

"And he carried to the wars with him a gilded
scutcheon, whereon he had no cognisance,
nor ordinary device of the Athenians,
but only had the image of Cupid on
it, holding lightning
in his hand."

Plutarch,
Lives

I LOOK
DIVINE

My BROTHER would not smile for a photograph. He smiled now and then in life, he was even known to laugh, but never for a camera. Even when we were growing up, when he was a little boy, Nicholas knew how he wanted to be seen.

He knew how he was willing to be remembered. Any camera would alert my brother's instinct for posterity.

In the years that we had grandmothers, one of them was the kind who liked to compose grandsons within a frame in front of a Christmas tree. She liked to pose the smaller boy in front of the bigger boy, the bigger boy holding the smaller one, me holding Nicholas, my arms around him, enfolding him from behind.

The idea, I think, was that this embrace would make us look like brothers.

Ours was a weak resemblance.

Nicholas would look at himself in the red glass ornaments hooked to the boughs, the ones that were silver inside when they shattered. He could see himself in them and in the presents wrapped in shining paper at our feet. He could find his face in the heaps of packages, of which more than half, every year, were invariably for him. He would be himself up to a point, as much as Nicholas ever was himself, until our grandmother would say, "Say *cheese.*"

We could not, even in those years, either of us, believe that we had that kind of grandmother.

Nicholas said that she came from a bad family.

He did not say this in those years; he said it later, in the years when he was fond of calling things *de trop*.

One year — almost thirty years ago — while we were waiting for the *cheese*, Nicholas stood on my shoes and reached behind us both. He put his hands in my back pockets and squeezed handfuls of me, the biggest handfuls he could get, clutching through the cloth. He held on to me, his feet planted on mine, and he tipped his weight forward, leaning with it, not to make us fall, but as though he wanted to take flight without leaving me behind.

I pulled him to me and smelled soap on his skin, starch in his white shirt, and the wool smell of his short gray trousers. I smelled tonic in his hair, and

Listerine, and under them, I was sure, I smelled our mother's perfume. It may have only been the scent that her kisses left behind, but with his weight on me I imagined Nicholas looking at himself in our mother's mirror, splashing her Arpège into his hand, then lavishing it behind his ears, as she did. I could picture my brother stroking perfume on the pulse of his neck, with the thrill that is the point of the forbidden.

I imagined what must have been his rapture.

I squeezed him tighter, and while our grandmother squinted, trying to attach the flash, Nicholas took one hand from inside my pocket and forced it in between us.

He whispered, "Goose you!"

I felt his laughter in my feet. I felt it rise, I felt his laughter in his ribs, where I was holding him. My brother's laughter made me laugh. I felt it in his body, then in mine.

I thought our grandmother should have captured *that*. I thought that would have been a picture worth taking, worth having.

It would be worth having now.

Now it would be proof.

Nicholas and I were still laughing when she told us she was ready.

She called us *boys*.

She said *cheese*.

"Cheese, boys," our grandmother said.

That was all it took to stop my brother's laughter. Nicholas stepped down from my shoes. He folded his hands in front of his body and made them mimic a boyish repose. I watched his face change in the ornaments.

He changed it to a face that he had taught himself. It was a face that a little boy will learn to make after hearing too often that he is a beautiful little boy, in the same way that children who have been told that they are smart are apt to teach themselves to act it.

It was a face that said, "This is how I look."

Our grandmother said that she was waiting for Nicholas to smile.

I kicked his foot and told him to do it. I told him that the smile would only be for her, that no one else would see it. I told him that it would not end up on the cover of *Photoplay* or anywhere else that would embarrass him.

I told him that a smile was nothing.

Nicholas stepped forward, a step away from me. Then he turned his face all the way around and gave me a look of everlasting patience that did not want to last.

"You are so *oblibious,"* he said. "How do I know who she's going to *show* it to?"

He kept looking at me, kept giving me the look, and there was nothing else to see. There was nothing else in his face that I could make out under the look, and it occurred to me then, posing with my brother thirty years ago, that standing in front of me was a seven-year-old boy who had already vowed to show the world only the face that he wanted it to see and had done so at a time while he was still negotiating speech.

He stepped back, finally, into my embrace, turned to the camera and offered the unsmiling face, until our grandmother gave in and took the picture of Nicholas posing in the way he was willing to be seen.

There is no photograph of my brother standing on my feet. There is no photograph of my brother laughing. In the photographs from those years, in every one of them, I am the brother in the back, the one who always looks like any boy who ever smiled for a grandmother.

Nicholas is the one who always looks like Nicholas.

This is the room I thought that I would start in, and for the past several hours I have stayed in it, sitting on my brother's unmade bed, without starting.

I could start anywhere. Any room would do.

I could empty ashtrays, open windows, take down pictures, put books in boxes, check the kitchen for spoiled food. I could throw out old onions.

I could flip through the mail that has kept coming and pitch the junk.

I could pick my brother's clothes up from the floor and try them on for fit, then go through drawers and feel under folded clothes, under lining paper, for things he might have hid there.

Music could help me start, then help me hurry. I could hum "Moon River."

That would be a record Nicholas would have. In another room, records fill a wall of shelves that do not stop until the ceiling. Everything that I could ever want to play or sing along to is here for me to play. I could pick out Broadway scores and belt out the big numbers over the stars who belt them on the records.

Or, as I used to see my brother do when he was a little boy, I could lip-synch in the mirror. I could close my eyes the way I used to watch him do, making them look closed but, I was always sure, keeping a space to look through, his eyelash space, so that he could see what he looked like with his eyes closed.

Nicholas used to do that.

I do not know for a fact that he stopped doing it.

He used to pretend that pencils were long cigarette holders and would glide around rooms flicking ashes into flowerpots, saying things like, "Daddy, don't be *droll*."

That is something else my brother used to do.

I cannot say that I am sure he ever stopped doing it.

I cannot say for certain that he did not know he was being watched.

I cannot even say that my brother did not know I was the one who was watching.

There might be another way. Maybe I could pay to get this done, pay someone to pack up and empty this place out. There must be companies you can call, the way you do when you move, companies that come with cartons, with padded wrap, and do it for you.

There must be a way to get it done, without doing it yourself.

There must be a way to get it all behind you.

If not, someone has not been smart, someone has not been on the ball. Someone has overlooked a need, missed a calling, lost a chance, because doing this could be an industry.

Doing this could be a life.

But I do nothing that a company would do. I stay here, sitting on the cashmere blanket with the cigarette burn in it, looking at objects around the room, my little brother's things as he left them.

Of course, I have looked a bit in other rooms, but I have chosen this room — if chosen it is what I've done — because this is the room with the best objects.

I do not mean "best" in the sense of necessarily to my taste, though I am thinking that I may take the lacquer table by the bed.

I can see myself in it.

Nicholas once told me the name for this kind of antique lacquer, for the old Japanese process that, over time, makes the black base show through in random patches under the red layers laid over it. The red is actually an orange-red, what is sometimes called Chinese red, but the name that Nicholas told me sounded Italian, not Japanese, not even Oriental, and it may have been that Nicholas did not know the real name.

Nicholas may have called it a name that the men who made it never called it.

I am wondering if Nicholas knew the name that the lacquer is called among the artisans. I am wondering if he ever got around to learning Japanese, as he used to threaten that he would one day, because he expected it would be fun to flirt with what he called little Japanese houseboys, what he called little Japanese comestibles.

Nicholas called most men little.

It was nothing against the Japanese.

Nicholas liked beautiful things. But he did not keep

them beautiful. The lacquer is water-ringed from drinks he drank in bed.

I mean "best" in another sense.

I mean "best" in the sense that objects, particulars, things like cigarette burns in cashmere blankets and water rings on antique lacquer, can be said to cast a verdict on a life.

I am not saying they do.

I am saying they can be said to.

I myself would be inclined to say they do.

Nicholas knew a few things about lacquer. Years ago, he told me what he knew.

Lacquer comes from toxic sap. The sap comes from a tree that is called by different names around the world. Actually, there are different species of the tree. In Japan, for example, there is the *Rhus verniciflua;* in Thailand, in Burma, there is the *Melanorrhoea laccifera.* The trees are somewhat different, but their sap, I understand, is more or less the same. When raw, if touched, the sap will burn through skin. The sap must take in oxygen to lose the poison and is slow to do so at high altitudes, though lacquer trees will grow high up. Lacquer trees will grow on mountains.

Sometimes the sap is mixed with ash, a vehicle for air. You will not often find lacquer that is pure.

The process that can force the black base through

was invented by monks, by accident. It made their temple rich, their discovery of how to simulate the aging. They learned how to hasten nature and make layers wear away as though time had done it.

They learned to make it happen on command.

I expect, though, that my brother's table is the real item, lacquer aged the valued way, before the monks learned to coax the base, by artifice, to come up through the many sheer layers of red.

This lacquer table was a present from a man. For a number of years in his life, Nicholas attracted many presents.

I must make a note to have it appraised.

I must make a note to inquire what can be done about the water rings.

There must be a gentle technique.

I will make my notes in a minute.

There are objects on the lacquer and also objects in it. On it are two glasses, a half-empty bottle of tequila, and a glass ashtray filled up to the top with cigarettes smoked down to the filters — different filters, one kind cork, one kind white — and many snapped nitrites mixed in among them.

The yellow box with the warning on it remains here by the bed.

I have not seen this kind, the old, snapping kind, for years. One sees the liquid now, in vials, if one sees anything. These are the kind that one can hardly buy now, hard to get, and there are more of them in this ashtray than I remember coming to a box.

I wonder — did Nicholas go through them, as it were, in one *sitting*, or did they, as things will, if allowed, accumulate?

I wonder if on nights he was alone, my brother looked at them, to remember nights that he had not been.

In the lacquer, I can see the underside of a dark linen lampshade, and up inside it, naked, the light-bulb it hides. I see picture frames, the pictures in them, prints of figures in kimonos, masked actors, courtesans, their blues and whites tinted by entrapment in the orange-red; and depending on where I move or how I lean, I can see, slanting in the flat surface, just up to the red obi tied tight around his waist, where the lacquer edge cuts it, the blown-up photograph of my brother posing, years ago, in a long black Japanese robe.

To see higher, to see the face, I need to look up from the lacquer to the wall, where it looks down, my brother's face, life-size within a mirrored frame.

Of course he does not smile.

In the mirrored frame, behind the light-splashed glass, my brother stands against a wall of skull-like faces carved in stone. His pose includes a cigarette, white filtered, and a hollow-stemmed champagne glass that he is holding to his neck, just below the jawline.

Nicholas prized his jawline; he prized all his bones.

The obi is tight around what was then a smaller-than-boyish waist.

A champagne bottle stands on a dried-out patch of grass at my brother's feet. The bottle is turned name-side to the camera and has a year on it. The year on the bottle, of course, would not be the year of the photograph. The year of the photograph would have been a proper year to drink the vintage. The proper year to drink a vintage is the kind of thing that Nicholas made it a point to know.

The bottle at my brother's feet is labeled 1962, and I would guess that it would have to be five or six years older than the photograph, at least, though this is not the kind of thing I make a point of knowing.

The cigarette between my brother's fingers is smoked to a photogenic length of ash and is held at an angle that was, even then, a dated way to hold a cigarette. But it is clear that Nicholas meant to feature his hands.

Someone must have told him that he had beautiful hands.

Nicholas did have beautiful hands, and the only word that I can think of for the way he holds the cigarette is, I am afraid, demure.

There are other words, of course, but demure will have to do.

What I wondered, until I realized that it was not a question, was why a thirty-seven-year-old man would have displayed, life-size in his bedroom, in sight of his bed, in a mirrored frame on a mirrored wall, and mirrored all around by other walls, a photograph of himself looking like a twenty-two-year-old boy, or even younger, nineteen, eighteen, because Nicholas spent most of his life looking younger than he was.

You may have noticed that this is often true of men over-cherished in childhood, common, for example, among favored sons — an exemption from the first shocks of aging that is a hallmark of the self-regarding.

We were seven years apart. Our mother and father had not been young when I was born; when Nicholas came, he was their miracle.

He came weeks before he should have, cut from our mother's stomach in a crisis that was not discussed.

I used to think he staged that entrance.

I used to imagine Nicholas coiled in our mother, pressing to get out, to get born and be adored, as though he knew that being born — too soon, sickly, delicate — was all that he would need to do in life. I know, of course, I knew even then, that there can be no sound in the womb, that life before birth is as without sound as life is after life, but I still imagined Nicholas crying out before his first breath to be made alive at once, beautiful at once, and adored without delay.

In fact, there are times I still imagine this. Today, for example, I can almost hear the cries. And in truth, nothing I imagine requires vast imagination: the womb would not have been too soon for Nicholas to demand his due.

For years, Nicholas would frequently remark that being born Caesarian was the next best thing to being adopted. I cannot say how many times I heard my brother say this.

One year, when we no longer had grandmothers, one of the years that our mother and father took us to Mexico every Christmas, I heard my brother tell a little boy his age, in the pool of the Cuernavaca Racquet Club, that Caesarian babies were more beautiful.

Nicholas explained to the little boy that being born in the usual way, through the mother, can deform a baby, make it ugly.

He made a face with his mouth and said, "Squish."

I watched my brother raise his arms from the water

to trace his wet mouth with his pool-wrinkled fingers. He traced his eyes and caressed, in both hands, the molding of his skull. Then, the proof exhibited, Nicholas explained to the little boy that Caesarian babies were more beautiful because they were more perfect.

Our mother was there, heard it all, and she told Nicholas that there was no such thing as *more perfect*.

She must have meant, of course, that there was no such English as more perfect, but that was not what she said, not the way she put it. What our mother told Nicholas when she looked up from a magazine to correct his grammar was that there was no such thing.

"Sweetheart," our mother said to Nicholas, "there is no such thing as *more perfect*."

Nicholas looked up at her and said, *"Of course there is."*

Then my brother asked the little boy, "How were you born?"

My brother liked to tell about the times that he had nearly died.

He talked about the epidemic of pneumonia that had killed babies in the hospital the week that he was born.

There *was* an epidemic that killed babies in the hospital the week Nicholas was born, but that epidemic was not pneumonia. I think it nearly killed Nicholas that what had nearly killed him was, in fact, another killer altogether. One drawback of being born too soon, weeks before he should have been, was that his birth coincided with a week in which many babies born in that hospital perished from an outbreak of what was, at the time, politely referred to as dysentery.

Nicholas was one of the babies saved with tea.

He hated that part of the story. He wanted some dignity in what he called his near-demise. He wanted to have nearly died of something tragic, poignant, stylish, chic.

First he made pneumonia up, then changed that to scarlet fever. He was partial for a while to scarlet fever, partial, that is, to scarlet fever as a thing to have nearly died from. When he learned that scarlet fever was frequently disfiguring, he took up poisoned blood.

He knew better than to be more specific; poisoned blood said all he wanted it to say.

He remained loyal to poisoned blood, until he discovered lactose intolerance.

Nicholas cherished lactose intolerance. He cherished, I think, the notion that his own infant body could have rejected the most basic nutrient. He must have also cherished the notion of carrying his near-death within his own system, the drama of an inborn cause, and he abandoned, I believe without reluctance, the range of the infectious for the sake of the innate.

In some versions of his near-deaths, my brother detailed his salvation by transfusion; in others, he had gasped for breath, for months, in incubation.

Years later, when he would tell his different versions to people we met traveling, when more or less complete strangers in hotel bars would ask if these narrow escapes from death had really happened, my brother had a fixed reply.

"How else, honey," Nicholas would ask, "do you think I'd be alive?"

When he first came home, saved by tea, our mother told me not to touch him. I thought of him as priceless, antique, Chinese — another museum piece in the house.

I touched him anyway. I blew on his face and watched his eyelids flutter. Between his eyes was a small blue vein to pinch. Once, when I pinched to hurt, he smiled right up at me, and I was sure that he was stupid.

A few years later, he nearly died again; that time, it *was* pneumonia.

Nearly dying was something my brother did well. Nicholas knew how to be cherished. He went on hunger strikes and had seizures. They were real, but

I always suspected that he knew how to bring them on. I was always sure that he knew how to fall down and go into a spasm at will, and I wondered why he did not look worse in a fit.

His was the minor affliction, the kind that children can grow out of, and he always looked unruffled in a spasm.

The face remained composed.

He looked rapturous.

He asked me once what he looked like in a fit. I told him he did not want to know. I knew he would ask again, and when he did, I touched him and told him that his eyes bulged out and rolled up white, that his skin turned red, and that his mouth was transformed into a huge, wide-open, beatific smile. I told him that the smile was so huge, so wide-open, you could see the tail wagging.

I told him this and watched his face collapse.

When Nicholas was twelve he was tested for intelligence. That test made him, all at once, a genius.

Becoming a genius took Nicholas one day.

As with my own test, no score was reported, no actual number. It was our father's idea to keep our scores from us. When I had my test, several years before Nicholas became a genius — when in fact

Nicholas was still learning to tie his shoes — our father called the two of us in to his dressing room and told us that what he had to say concerned us both. Nicholas stood in a corner, leaning into it, looking unconcerned, and that was the expression he more or less maintained when our father announced that I was an intelligent boy.

I already knew I was; he had told me this before, but this time I was smart enough to know that he was talking about the test, my test.

Nicholas was also smart enough to know this. He knew that there had been a test, that I had had it and he had not.

Our father was changing for dinner and sat down in a wing chair to take off his shoes. When he bent over to untie them, Nicholas moved from the corner to the doorway. From a remarkably early age Nicholas was partial to standing in doorways, or more accurately, he was partial to doorways as places to stand. Among places to stand, Nicholas tended to prefer settings to locations. Doorways, of course, are settings.

They are also frames. When my brother moved from a corner of our father's dressing room into the doorway in the same instant that our father bent over to untie his shoes, he did so, I realized, with an instinct for placing himself in a frame.

Our father looked at both of us and said that young

boys, if they know their scores and if their scores are high, will be too eager to repeat them. He pointed a shoehorn at me and said that nothing was more distasteful than this. To do this, he told me, to repeat the actual number, was as distasteful, as unbecoming to a gentlemen, as to volunteer one's net worth in the course of general conversation. Then, having a thought, our father shook his head forlornly and said that it was his experience along these lines that men who insist on telling numbers tend to tell numbers that are nothing much to tell.

I knew all this. But I wanted to know how smart I was. I promised that I would not repeat the number, but our father did not answer. He undid his tie, then his belt, signs that Nicholas and I had been excused.

I was about to leave, but I could see that Nicholas was not. When our father's back was turned, I saw my brother step on his own shoelaces to untie them with his feet. It did not take him any time to do it, and then he stayed in the doorway and made his face look like a little boy who could not tie his shoes.

That was the face that our father saw in the doorway when he told us we could go, and it was with that face that Nicholas looked up at our father, then down at his shoes, and said, "Teach me again, Daddy."

Our father told me I could go. I left the room but stayed just outside. The cracking sounds I heard meant that our father had gone down on his knees to show my brother one more time how to tie a shoelace. I could picture our father on his knees at my brother's feet, but more than that I pictured Nicholas standing over him, perhaps not even looking down to watch what our father's hands were doing.

I had barely formed that picture when I heard my brother whisper to our father, "Daddy, what's the number?"

When Nicholas was tested, he was not called in to our father's dressing room. Nicholas was called in to the library, and so was our mother, and so was I.

My brother's score did not occasion a father-son talk. My brother's score occasioned a conference. In that conference, no number was disclosed, nor was any mention made of what was unbecoming to a gentleman. In the conference that his score occasioned, there was talk about Nicholas being as smart as any child in California.

Our mother's version was that Nicholas's score was so high, they did not have a score for it. Her version was that it was too astonishing to measure.

Mine apparently was not.

A few times, I tried to get our mother to tell me my score. One time I nearly got it out of her. She said she could tell me, but that it would be unfair for me to have a number when Nicholas did not. It would be wrong, she said, for only one of us to know.

But once, when we were getting new suits, when Nicholas and I were standing together in a mirror being measured for cuffs, I heard our mother tell another woman that both her sons were brilliant, but that her younger son, the little one, was *more* brilliant. I heard our mother whisper numbers to the woman, and I was sure that the number she gave Nicholas was a number she'd made up.

Nicholas's did not sound like a number for intelligence.

It sounded like a number for Nicholas.

But I believed the number that was mine.

To accept my brother as a genius took an effort that was more than I could take. The notion struck me as nonsense. But when our mother and father told him that he was one, Nicholas did something smart.

He pretended not to believe it, not to be impressed. He acted shy about it, made himself act modest. This was smarter than it sounds, because in order to act modest Nicholas first had to figure out how a modest person acts.

He must have known that this was the lovable thing to do.

I am not sure that if it had been me, I would have been smart enough to pretend, to make myself so lovable. Pretending like that — being lovable like that — may be the kind of thing that it takes a little genius to do.

His modesty was almost convincing, but I knew it was an act. I knew him. I went to a library and read up on the theory of the testing. I read what it was the scores meant, and the next time I was home, after I had finished my research, I went into my brother's room one night and told him that the highest possible score could not make him any more than twice as good as average.

This came close to the facts, as I had noted them.

I watched his face while I told him. He was stretched out on his bed, surrounded by our mother's magazines. The layout he had open featured fur coats. Our mother had dog-eared the page. Nicholas began to flatten down the fold, gave up, turned the page, examined a new fur, and, finally, looked up at me.

I could tell that he wanted me out of the room while he thought about being, at best, nothing more spectacular than twice as good as average. I knew that he wanted to hide, that he wanted no witness to his little death.

Nicholas looked down again at the furs.

Nicholas had brown eyes which, in many lights, looked black. He had extravagant black lashes that looked false, and dark hair that even in those years he was allowed to grow so long that he could drag his fingers through it and take almost forever to come out at the end.

That is what he did then, that gesture. He pulled his fingers through his hair, raked it off his face.

"Who cares what it means," he said, "as long as it's as high as you can go?"

Then, as though I were not in the room, he turned to a new page of furs with florid languor.

I did not leave. I stayed and watched him while he pretended to be absorbed in the furs. He pretended to read an article in French. His hands looked trapped in his hair.

I told him brains develop in the womb, that by being born too soon he had probably lost points. I did not know if this was true, but I watched it sinking in; I watched Nicholas believing it.

Finally, he looked up at me and said what he always did when he had had more of me than he could take.

He sighed, "Oh, go to your womb."

Much later that night, I heard my brother through his door, whispering to himself. He must have been studying his face in the mirror when I heard him whisper, "You are the smartest little boy in the world, and you also look like this."

I have pushed the table forward with my feet to see my brother's face inside the lacquer.

The sight of cigarettes and nitrites piled up in the glass ashtray made me want to empty it, to clean it, get it to sparkle, get it immaculate — and get a cigarette and light up.

I did all that; now the ashtray is as full as it was.

It is getting dark outside; in this room it's getting late. I have cleaned the glasses by the bed and am about to drink what is left of the tequila. I want the bottle out of the room, away from the bed. This is a small matter, I admit, but I do not like liquor bottles in bedrooms. It is not that I have rules against drinking in bed; on the contrary, I have taken many drinks to bed. But what I take is the drink — the liquor in the glass. To make another drink, I leave the bed; I put on a robe and take the glass to the bottle, in another room. Unless I have cleared some messy evenings from my mind — which is possible, of course, but which I do not believe to be the case — I can claim truthfully that taking a liquor bottle into a bedroom is something I have never done, and which I, unlike Nicholas, would be incapable of doing.

Also unlike Nicholas, I keep a pair of coasters on the table by my bed.

On the other hand, it is unlikely that I would discard a crushed nitrite ampoule so neatly in an ashtray. This is another thing that I am wondering tonight:

how it could be that a man who would burn cigarette holes in a cashmere blanket and leave water marks on antique lacquer would, presumably in a state of some abandon, reach across a bed, perhaps across a body, to deposit crushed, sniffed nitrites in a bedside ashtray. In a state of abandon, I might have dropped them on the sheet or stuffed them for the time being into a pillowcase.

Of course, this is hard to say for sure; I have not used the things for years.

And of course, it might not have been Nicholas who put them in the ashtray.

It might have been the other man, being fastidious.

I try the window, to open it, but I breathe through the glass instead, because there is nothing to breathe outside but night. Down below, a late-fifties convertible with tail fins has stopped for a red light. When the light does not change, the car races off, and when it is gone, I can still hear this year's music coming out of it. Years ago, in parking lots, on highways, Nicholas used to sing "Swing Low, Sweet Cadillac." He used to say that cars with fins made him believe it could be possible to get far enough away.

Across the street, storefront windows all along the block display men's clothes for the fall. In a few months it will be time for the scarves tucked into overcoats. Now it is time to look. It is always time to look.

Of course Nicholas would live across the street from a showcase of adornment, from male mannequins posed in artificial light. Leather jackets are slung over shoulders or ballooned around perfections of torso; trousers are belted tight around improbable frugalities of waist. From his bed, Nicholas could look down upon an avenue of waxy cheekbones, a prohibition of repose.

As a little boy, Nicholas called men's clothes frocks. He must have seen the word somewhere, perhaps in one of our mother's magazines, or he might have heard the word from her, though it was not a word she used, or from a movie, from one of the thirties comedies that thrilled him. He might have heard the word from an actress with a cigarette holder.

When he first said it, it is possible that he did not know what he was saying.

Years later, when he did know what he was saying, Nicholas said that he had learned about life from Rosalind Russell.

The first time I heard him use the word, I tried to tell him it was not a word to use. I meant, of course, that it was inappropriate, but what I said, the way I put it, was that boys did not wear frocks.

The look he gave me said that I was not good enough to give a look to. I had seen his face and the faces he put on it for more than half my life, and I had never seen the face that he put on it for the sake of frocks. That is how far Nicholas would go for a word he liked, for something he wanted to say, and that face is more or less the face I'm seeing tonight, the face that shines up at me twenty-five years later in the lacquer. In the mouth, in the unsmiling lips, in the dark eyes that look black in this light, I see my brother, I see Nicholas, giving me a look.

Some of the clothes that Nicholas called frocks were mine. He liked to put on my clothes in secret. He adored the shirts that could almost fit him twice, the sweaters that hung down on him like coats. He adored the trousers that came up to his ribs. One time he stole my belts and punched a hole in every one of them to make each one fit his waist.

He loved to wear the belts tight in the big trousers and roll up my cuffs and look at himself looking small.

I think Nicholas had a terror of size, of flesh, his own flesh, a terror of it. I think he would have been happier to have had no body, to have been no more than his face.

I could not stop him from putting on my clothes. I think wearing my clothes was his way of telling himself that he would always be younger, smaller, and that he would never not be cherished.

Once I saw him touching a pair of trousers on my bed. He reached down into the empty pockets, as if he would find something in them if he could reach inside them far enough, if not one time, then the next. He went from pocket to pocket in a cycle, turning my trousers front to back. He looked as though he thought each pocket would be something new each time it came around.

I stood behind the door and watched my brother reach down into my pockets. I could not believe that he would do it again — and then he would do it again. I made bets with myself about how many times he would do it. I bet that if he did it three more times we would become orphans; our mother and father would die together in a plane and make us rich.

I made a bet that every time he reached into my pockets there would be another fortune to divide.

I made a bet that if he reached in five more times, he would die, too, and I would get the fortune to myself, but that if he did it five more times after that, I would die instead, and Nicholas would be the one to stay behind and drown in all the fortune.

When I made that bet, I stopped betting. Not dying, drowning in fortune, sounded like the kind of luck that Nicholas would have. That bet sounded like my brother's life.

I thought that one more bet could be the end of everything but him.

Many years ago, a woman at a garden party given by our mother asked Nicholas what he was going to be when he grew up.

Nicholas answered that he would not have to be anything. He told the woman that his mother and father were old and would die before he grew up. He told her they would leave him money, that when he grew up he was going to be rich. He told the woman that he was rich already from his grand-mothers. Nicholas pointed to me and told the woman that we were both already richer, worth more, than our father. He said that we were worth more than our mother. We were richer, my brother told the woman, worth more, than our mother and our father put together. He told the woman that when our mother and father died we would be even richer.

Nicholas said, "*More* richer."

There was no mistaking his delight. He did not need to smile to make his delight clear.

The woman told Nicholas that when boys grow up they have to be something. Even rich boys, the woman said, when they grow up, no matter how rich they are, have got to be something. Nicholas looked at the woman appraisingly, and said, "Not if they're smart, they don't."

The woman insisted. She said that no matter how rich or how smart, boys had to be something. She said all boys had to.

Nicholas told the woman it was time for him to circulate.

Hours later, when the party was over and the guests had gone, I heard the woman's voice in my doorway.

"Boys have to be something."

I looked up from my bed, surprised the woman had not left, and I saw that her voice was not coming from her: it was not the woman who was speaking. It was Nicholas posing in the doorway, speaking with her voice.

He had turned his voice into the woman's voice exactly.

I asked him to do it again.

He did. He repeated, word for word I think, every-thing that the woman had said in the garden, and every cadence was flawless, every syllable precise.

"All right," Nicholas went on in the woman's voice. "If I have to be something, I think I shall be capti-vating."

That afternoon, twenty-five years ago, my brother gave, first to the woman in the garden, then later to me, a more or less visionary forecast of his life. What he said would happen did happen. Before he grew up he did find himself rich, and it is more than likely that he found himself captivating.

I have found a glass like the one in the photograph and have poured out the last of the tequila.

From the foot of the bed it is possible to look into a wall of mirrors and see the photograph of my brother in the Japanese robe and the display of mannequins across the street mirrored together in such a way that Nicholas appears to be among them.

He does not appear to be one of them. The mannequins across the street do not hold cigarettes at angles to feature their hands, and the mannequins across the street do not wear Japanese robes. The mannequins across the street are grouped around stationary bicycles and chrome masses of exercise equipment. Only a few of the mannequins across the street wear anything that Nicholas would have called a frock. Those that do, those in cashmere or angora, are displayed in the process of taking those clothes off. The mannequins across the street shrug themselves from coat sleeves; they pull belts through loops; they bend down to untie shoes, all of this in order, presumably, to join the other mannequins, the shirtless ones in gym shorts bunched up at the crotch.

The shirtless mannequins across the street in the

windows that Nicholas could see from his bed are hanging from chin-up bars, or they are wedged into apparatus to give the impression of straining for all that they are worth.

I look at Nicholas among the mannequins.

Nicholas is posing for all that he is worth.

Nicholas never spoke about his body. Nicholas spoke about his figure. I think that Nicholas's idea of physical exertion, if he had one, would have been to take a taxi to a gym and smoke a cigarette in the locker room. I wonder if it ever occurred to him, at any time since the photograph was taken, the years that he could look out and see the standards change from season to season in the windows, that the ideal young beauty captured in the pose, even if he could have kept it, had ceased to be ideal. I wonder if it crossed his mind that being captivating had ceased to be the fashion, or sufficient.

I study the angle of the cigarette and the bare feet crossed under the border of the Japanese robe. Even the feet are posed. It must have killed Nicholas that he did not have beautiful feet. Nicholas had, in fact, enormous feet. Nothing else was wrong with them, but they were enormous for the rest of him, and I expect they are the reason for the champagne bottle positioned on the grass. I expect that the bottle is there to hide the feet as much as possible.

I am trying to be sure about the setting, to know

where, exactly, he is standing, to remember trips I know he took. In his teens, in his twenties, my brother's life became a travelogue. Some of the trips he took, he took with me. I became, in the legal sense, his guardian, also his trustee. For the first five years after our mother and father died, when I had moved out and Nicholas lived alone in the house we had grown up in, I bought him trips with my trustee fee. I could, of course, have waived a trustee fee, but Nicholas said that I should take it. Nicholas always said the worst things in life are free. After our father and our mother died, it was his idea to keep going to Mexico every year for Christmas.

He said life goes on.

One of those times in Mexico, on a Christmas Eve in Mérida, in a bar in a hotel where the band was playing the kind of music that hotel bars in Mérida tend to play on Christmas Eve, Nicholas shouted over the music to a man who had joined us and expatiated for the man's reluctant benefit on the distinctions between *élan* and *panache*.

Nicholas remarked that the man had *élan,* but that he did not have *panache.* I was not sure that Nicholas might not have meant it the other way around, but I was useless that night for distinctions. I had been drinking everything that night. The man without *panache* had bought us many rounds. I ordered drinks I never drink. I got a thirst for sidecars and grasshoppers and golden cadillacs. I got a thirst for them so that the man would have to say their names when he ordered them for me. Their names made him wince. You can get some pretty funny grasshoppers in Mérida, but I did not care how bad they were. I tried, without success, to get a pousse-café.

The man would not leave Nicholas alone. He would not stop talking about what he must have meant to call my brother's *joie de vivre,* except that what came out was *suave de vivre.*

"You've got *suave de vivre,* kid," the man kept telling Nicholas.

I thought I knew what the man meant, but I had no idea what Nicholas meant by *panache.* At the time, however, my brother's observation of his lack of it struck me as an uncanny diagnosis of what I disliked about the man.

"You have no *panache,* " Nicholas told the man, "but I adore your tum-tum."

The man had a bit of a stomach, nothing monstrous, but there was some protuberance, and I sat at the table and watched Nicholas reach inside the man's shirt to rub his stomach. He kept telling the man that he adored it.

"I just adore your tum-tum," Nicholas told the man. "With this tum-tum, you don't need *panache.* With this tum-tum, you don't even need *élan.*"

The fact was that Nicholas could not possibly have

adored the man's stomach. The fact was that Nicholas had a revulsion to excess flesh. To avoid having it himself, in fact, Nicholas frequently took ipecac. I could not tell whether my brother was going out of his way to be kind to the man, or going further not to be, but watching Nicholas rub the man's stomach under his shirt that night made me feel almost sorry for the man. Anyone could tell how much the poor fool loved it.

The next day I asked Nicholas how, given his revulsion, he could have brought himself to put his hand on the man's stomach.

We were at a table, and Nicholas picked up a knife to look at his face. He checked his eyes for bloodshot. His eyes, of course, were not bloodshot. His eyes, in those years, were never bloodshot.

"I've got *suave de vivre*," he said.

In the years that his life was a travelogue Nicholas had what he called his favorite places in the world. He would say of one place or another that it was his favorite in the world, the one place he loved more than any other, though there were, in fact, quite a few places that Nicholas claimed to love more than any other. The places that Nicholas claimed to love more than any other tended to be indoors and to be, in one way or another, mercantile. The places that Nicholas called his favorite in the world were places where clothes or drinks or objects could be bought, and where people could be seen wearing or drinking or buying them. They tended, actually, to be places that one could know about and even claim to love, if one wanted to, without necessarily having been to them.

For a few years Nicholas's favorite place in the world was the bar off the lobby of the Ritz in Madrid. He was partial especially to the skylight ceiling and to the light that he said came through it in the summer between seven-thirty and nine o'clock in the evening. He said that it was the best light for bone structure, and he appreciated, too, that men were not admitted without jackets and ties. Nicholas maintained that God had not yet made the man who did not look better in a jacket and a tie. What he meant was that he preferred men in expensive clothes. In those years, and maybe still, the bar off the lobby of the Ritz in Madrid was frequented between seven-thirty and nine o'clock in the evening by men who were not staying at the Ritz. There were tables where you could sit on low couches or chairs, and Nicholas held it as an axiom that there was no one who did not look better on a low couch or chair than on a barstool. It was, specifically, one of those low tables that was his favorite place in the world, and there

were two weeks in a summer nineteen years ago —
the year, in fact, on the bottle in the photograph —
during which we found ourselves every evening at
that table.

That table was for four or six, not for two, and
when the bar was busy, which between seven-thirty
and nine o'clock it tended to be, other people would
come to sit with us at that table.

One night, we were joined by two young Amer-
ican men in military uniforms. The two young men
had crew cuts, were a few years older than Nicholas,
and both were enormous examples of what they were.
They sat in the low chairs with their legs wide apart
and exuded, both of them, an expansive physical ease
that was blatant.

Nicholas began to whisper his part of our conversation. I did not know why, but I began to whisper,
too. We sat together on the couch, at the low table,
whispering. I do not think either of us cared what
we talked about. I think we both wanted to hear the
huge young men.

Nicholas made a point of turning to the side. He
leaned toward me in a way that he must have meant
to look intimate and conspiratorial, and it did look
intimate, and it looked conspiratorial. There were
times in public when Nicholas did not act toward me
like a brother, times when it suited him not to treat

me as one. That night in the bar off the lobby of the Ritz in Madrid was one of those times. That night Nicholas whispered to me out of his profile. He lowered his head to an angle that he must have believed to be his most becoming.

It was becoming, and he did something with his eyes that made them look animated, a thing I always hated when he did it. It was a trick he had of looking up at someone while his face was looking down, so that the lower part of his eyes would turn up white. He must have thought it was alluring.

It was alluring, but I always hated it when he made himself alluring with me.

The huge young men in crew cuts did not acknowledge us. They sat with their legs wide apart and talked for a while about the bullfights they had seen that afternoon. After a while, they began to plan their evening. One of them, the one who was maybe not as huge as the other, wanted to see more bullfights, but the other one, the one who was maybe even bigger, told his friend that Madrid had no bullfights at night. He said there was nothing to do but go to dinner, eat some eels, and after that they could try a place he'd heard about, a nightclub he called it, where, he told his friend, female contortionists danced.

When the one who was maybe even bigger said

that, the one who was disappointed about the bull-fights shifted in his chair in such a way that Nicholas had to turn and look.

I had to, too. I could not help it, either.

Then the even bigger one also shifted in his chair, spread his legs apart even wider, and it was hard to decide which one of them to look at.

Still in profile, Nicholas leaned toward me and whispered, "Bless their hearts, these big ones."

The one who was disappointed about the bull-fights became sullen and told the one who had proposed the nightclub that they could go to dinner, but he did not know about the nightclub. He did not know about the nightclub, he said, because he had to think about the time change. He had to think about the time change because he had to call Florida.

"I've got to call Mom," said the one who was maybe not as huge.

When Nicholas heard that, he turned face-front in the couch. He spread his legs apart as far as he could spread them, leaned toward the men across the table, and in a voice I had not heard from him before, a deep, forceful voice that was not his, he spoke to the huge young men directly.

"Fuck Mom," Nicholas said.

The two huge young men stared across the table at Nicholas. The one who had to call Florida brought his knees together and cupped his hands in his lap.

"Go *see* those female contortionists," Nicholas said in the unknown voice to the young men in crew cuts and military uniforms that night in the bar off the lobby of the Ritz in Madrid. "Go see those female contortionists *dance.*"

A week later Nicholas was still talking about the huge young men in crew cuts.

"Bless their hearts," he said. "They wanted to do their own contortions, but there was nothing to do but eat some eels."

Nicholas was always blessing men's hearts.

Once he blessed the heart of a man in a river.

It was a man he never met, never spoke to, but whom we saw together once, a lean, finely made man stripped to the waist, rowing a one-man craft one late morning, in summer, in Rome, in the Tiber.

Together, we watched the man rowing.

He was *so* finely made.

Ordinarily, we would have watched him from a bridge and would not have seen as closely as we did how finely made he was. In Rome, the bridges are high above the river, unusually so, as are the streets, the buildings, the city itself. If we had watched the man from so high up, we would have seen him, I think, as any man, rowing in any narrow river, anywhere; we would not have seen what he became for us.

For both of us.

But we did not see him from a bridge; we saw him almost from the river itself, from one of the broad, paved walks that curve along its banks, nearly level to the water when the river runs high. Down there, so far below the city, the river seems unrelated to it, and to walk down there between the bridges is like a short trip out of town. Looking up, you can see the bridge that you came down from, but no other reminders of the city, no buildings, no people, no streets. Now and then you may see the tops of tall elm trees that line the *lungotevere*, but you will seldom, if ever, hear the traffic on those boulevards above the river. You will seldom hear anything, though you are walking along a river that cuts through the center of one of the noisiest cities on this earth. To walk along the Tiber is an escape from Rome, right in the heart of it. Yet it is an escape that no one seems to take; you can almost always have it to yourself, solitude in the middle of the city, and having a part of Rome so completely to yourself, you feel Rome is yours.

That is the feeling I had that late morning when we saw the man rowing.

I think Nicholas had it, too. We were, both of us, more with the river than we were with each other, and we were not talking when we saw the man rowing. It was too quiet to speak.

When we saw him, we watched in silence until he rowed under a bridge, out of view.

Then Nicholas went on looking — at the river, everywhere the man had rowed, at where his oars had been.

He said, "I have got to swim in this river right now."

I told him he did not. I told him he could live without swimming in the river. He would be wise, I told him, to make himself live without swimming in the river.

"Stop being you," he said.

I suggested that no one swam in the river, that there were reasons no one did. For instance, I told him, the water itself. I told him to look at the water, at what it was and what was growing in it. The current, too. I told him it was stronger than it looked.

Nicholas was already taking off his clothes.

He may have thought that he was taking a dip in the Tiber, and of course he was, but it could not have been absent from his mind that he was also taking off his clothes in the middle of Rome.

"Don't look at me," he said, "until I'm in the river."

I said I was not going to look at him when he was *in* the river.

"Yes, you are," he said.

I tried to think of diseases that he could get from the water.

"You may watch me jump in," he said. "I don't mind if you see me from the back."

I had meant what I said about not looking; I had nothing in my mind when I changed it.

His hair came down his back, almost to his shirt-tail. He was still wearing his shirt. I should have known that Nicholas would swim in the Tiber with his shirt on.

Even with his back to me, I could tell that my brother was striking a pose. I was sure that he knew how his back looked.

I named diseases. I did not know if he could get them from the water, but at least they were diseases.

Typhoid, I said.

Malaria, I said.

Nicholas turned his face, showed me his profile over his shoulder.

One of his profiles, one of his shoulders.

"Honey," he said, "it's only life."

He unbuttoned his sleeves and jumped into the river. He had never learned to dive. I could not see him in the river until his head came up. Then his head was there, his face, but I could not see his body. The river was too dark to see below the surface.

It was only his face above the water. His hair floated out, blacker than the water, black spread out on black.

At first, he kicked against the current, swimming in the places where the man had rowed. When he had put himself in many of them, all the places we had seen him, he gave in to the current and drifted with it, back through the same places, toward a bridge downriver.

I followed his hair, his drifting face. I walked to the bridge where his body would emerge. He would come up the steps from the river to the walk. I carried his trousers, his shoes, a ball of linen socks.

I followed my brother drifting.

The places where the man had rowed were his.

"Seventeen years ago I sprang to life in this hotel," I remember hearing my brother tell a man from San Francisco, in the bar in the garden of the Hassler hotel, a few nights after he took the swim in the Tiber, in 1966.

We spent an amount of time in hotel bars. Nicholas was partial to hotel bars. I was, too. I cannot say that now and then I did not share his taste.

The man from San Francisco was with a woman, but Nicholas did not address himself to her. Nicholas seldom addressed himself to women. He tended to avoid conversations that did not hold at least a possibility of conquest. For Nicholas, when he traveled with me, conquest was mostly an unmessy affair, a flirtation returned, although his flirtations themselves could get somewhat lubricious. For flirtations, they could get a little gamy.

By "sprang to life," Nicholas must have meant to convey to the man from San Francisco a more vivacious image of human conception than could be achieved by clinical terms, but the man did not appear to get his meaning and obliged my brother to say, "I mean, I was conceived here, in this hotel, seventeen years ago, just upstairs."

"Just upstairs," the man from San Francisco repeated, as if a further meaning might be decoded epistrophically.

Actually, Nicholas had not "sprung to life" seventeen years before at the Hassler, "just upstairs." He had not "sprung to life" anywhere seventeen years before, not in any hotel, not anywhere in Rome, nor for that matter anywhere in Europe. Nicholas, I expect to his displeasure, had not been conceived "abroad." Twenty-two years before, Nicholas had been conceived in a large Victorian house, most likely on a large Victorian bed, possibly *in* the large Victorian bed, possibly under the covers, on Russian Hill, on Francisco Street, in the 800 block, where from our mother and father's large Victorian bed, as from all the rooms in front, there was a somewhat banal, postcard view of Alcatraz, which, when he was five, Nicholas found an affront and asked our father to have moved. I go into these details only to suggest that there was nothing unbecoming about the truth, about the actual site of my brother's conception. In other words, Nicholas "sprang to life" at a suitable address, but not suitable enough for Nicholas, not that night in Rome with the man from San Francisco, and since the notion of springing to life in the Hassler was a notion that pleased him, he embellished his biography to entertain the man.

He entertained himself, too, and that night with the man from San Francisco my brother began what became a tradition of attributing his conception to the leading hotels of the world.

He sprang to life at the Cipriani.

He sprang to life at the San Domenico Palace.

He sprang to life at the Royal Hawaiian.

As for the matter of chronology — the truncation of five years from his life, which he could get away with that year — Nicholas frequently remarked that there is no point in telling a lie that is only part untrue.

When people ask, I think I will say that my brother came to a bad end at the Crillon.

At Dukes.

The Ritz.

He would like that — coming to a bad end at a suitable address.

Even if it is a lie that is only part untrue.

"You should know that I never buy my second drink," my brother told the man from San Francisco.

It had come out that the man and woman were brother and sister instead of husband and wife.

The man bought Nicholas a drink. He bought me a drink and his sister a drink, and he bought himself one, too.

"Aren't we lucky," Nicholas said to the sister, "that we're stunning enough to get men to buy us drinks?"

By addressing this to the woman, Nicholas was, of course, addressing the man. It was the man who had been meant to hear it, and had. The woman, the sister, in her appearance, was unfortunate. The man was about my age, somewhat robust, built a little wide for double-breasted. I thought I might have seen him, here or there, before.

"It's lucky to be stunning," Nicholas went on. "I adore having drop-dead bone structure."

He turned to me, though I would not say he gave me his attention. He asked when I had first learned that I was stunning enough to get men to buy me drinks.

It was a topic I did not feel inclined to pursue in

front of the woman from San Francisco, and even less so in front of the man. I replied, to end the matter, that it was not a thing I'd learned, it was what I'd always known. I said that everyone ever born should be stunning enough at least once in his life to be bought a drink by someone.

The sister, who had made a dour face when Nicholas asked me the question, kept making it after I had answered.

"I had to learn," Nicholas said to me, but really to the man. "I was twelve years old, having a Coke at the Empress of China. I did not usually have Cokes at the Empress of China, and I don't think they encouraged children at their bar, but I'd been having lunch with my mother, our mother, and in the middle of cashew chicken she said she had to run an errand. She told me to wait for her at the bar. So I went to the bar when they brought the tea. I loathe tea. All my life I have loathed tea. So I was sitting at the bar of the Empress of China at three in the afternoon, and the only other person there was a little Japanese man, a darling little businessman in a seersucker suit. I mean the blue-and-white-striped kind, not the gray-and-white or brown-and-white, and he asked me, this little Japanese man, if I would like to taste his Scotch.

"You know, take a sip. A quick sip was what he

had in mind. He said we could be discreet, that no one need be the wiser. I remember very clearly that he said no one need be the wiser.

"He was so furtive about it, so sort of clandestine, I knew I shouldn't take a sip of his Scotch, so I told him that he could order a martini for himself, that I would drink it, and no one need be the wiser.

"Of course, I didn't think he'd do it. But he did. He ordered a martini and set it next to me and watched me drink it. That's all he did, he just watched me drink it, nothing else, except that two or three times while I was drinking it, he reached down into his trousers, I assumed to make some minor adjustments."

Listening to him, I could not place what it was that struck me as unlikely in my brother's anecdote. Something seemed off, but before I could pick it out the sister began to recommend things to see in Rome. She told us to make a point of seeing things we had already made a point of, mostly churches and church art. She was a woman who would recommend that one make it a point to see the Vatican. She made it clear that she had made up her mind about Nicholas and me, that we had not seen these things, that we were people who came to world capitals just to drink at good hotels.

She especially recommended a mural in Trastevere. She called it "Scenes from the Life of the Virgin."

I didn't know if the artist had called it that or if someone else had later, but I was pretty sure that Nicholas and I had seen it. Not that I could tell from the woman's description. She knew more about it than one could learn just by looking. She talked facts, talked technique; her description did not describe a thing that one could see. But she went on in a flat, unanimated voice, and as she did, I felt as if I was being read aloud to from a travel book, and not one that was first-rate. She knew more about the mural than I wanted to know, more than I wanted to hear, and I could tell that it was becoming more than Nicholas could bear.

"God help me," my brother said to the man from San Francisco, "if I see one more Virgin Mary, I'm going to get knocked up."

It must have been my brother's tone that set the woman off. I cannot say that his tone had nothing in it to offend. The woman looked across the table at my brother and told him that she could not help it, she just had to say that he was the most affected creature she had ever come across.

That was her word; she called him a creature. She inflected the word by not inflecting it at all.

She made it a point to say it without style.

That the woman from San Francisco had just had to say this to him did not seem to come as a surprise to Nicholas.

"Of course, you can't help it," my brother said to the woman. "Of course, you have to say it."

I noticed, because there was no way not to, that Nicholas was surpassing the woman in flatness of voice. He was far surpassing her. I had thought until then that I had heard my brother speak in every voice he had, even voices he did not, but I had not heard the voice that he was using with the woman. I had not before heard speech so stripped of ornament.

I told the woman that we had already seen the Scenes from the Life of the Virgin. I even called it that.

"Sweetheart, she doesn't care what we've seen," Nicholas said. He leaned forward, facing the woman across the table.

"I expect you pride yourself on being unaffected," my brother said to the woman.

"I do," the woman said.

"I don't," my brother said. "But I wonder all the time, who are people trying to fool, when they go through all their lives just acting like themselves."

He paused because he had come to a pause. After the pause, he said, "A little affectation now and then is just a little generosity."

That night, listening to my brother's unornamented voice in the garden above the Spanish Steps, it crossed my mind to consider what he'd said, and even as I tried to, even as I made a note to ask him later what he'd meant, I became aware that I would be unlikely anytime soon to shake off the image that had come to me of a Japanese businessman in a seersucker suit making minor adjustments at the Empress of China.

When the hotel bar began to close, long after his sister had excused herself, the man from San Francisco recommended a place open late, where, he told us, we could see the most beautiful men in Rome.

"They're all the most beautiful," Nicholas said when we were there.

"They think so, too," said the man from San Francisco.

Nicholas was right — every young man in the place could have passed himself off as the most beautiful in Rome. And the man from San Francisco was right that they all knew it.

It was a place where men could dance together, and most of the men were dancing, but not together.

There were no pairs; there were mirrors.

There were mirrors on walls, on columns, and the most beautiful men in Rome were dancing alone, each one by himself, watching himself, entranced with himself.

The men made eye contact with their own eyes.

The one wall not covered by mirrors was covered instead by a mural of opulently muscled, overgendered men, half or more undressed. The illustrator must have tried to capture how men might look if they could issue directly from each other in a womanless world, and in the mural the lewdly virile specimens, cartoon ideals, regarded each other with untender admiration.

The men on the dance floor, the most beautiful in Rome, did not regard each other at all. There was humor in the mural, in the illustrator's spirited excess. It was clear about the men in the mural that, made flesh, they would adore being what they would be. But the men on the dance floor gave no appearance of enjoying their beauty. Abandoned to self-study, their faces were intent, critical, unamused.

Nicholas looked at me and put my thought into words I might have chosen if he had not beat me to them.

"If you're going to fancy yourself, you should have some fun with it," he said.

"Look at them," the man from San Francisco said.

"They're lovely, of course," Nicholas said, "but I don't find them all that tasty. They're too dapper, too aesthetic, they're too effete for words. Actually, I find them epicene."

The men dancing in the mirrors *were* somewhat on the dapper side, and it could be said that they were more beautiful than handsome, but they could not accurately be called epicene. I realized, though, why my brother had. It was not only true that they were not looking at each other; it was also the truth that, when they danced by themselves in mirrors the most beautiful men in Rome were not looking at Nicholas.

It was a night that he was looking his best and he knew it. He was sitting between two older, good-enough-looking men at a front table, in several hundred dollars' worth of clothes, and the most beautiful men in Rome were not looking at his drop-dead bone structure, and it was not going over.

It was not going over, and it did not go over when the man from San Francisco got up to dance, to join the most beautiful men in Rome.

Nicholas watched the man claim a mirrored column.

It did not go over.

Nicholas watched the man from San Francisco dance by himself.

"Screw him," I said to my brother. "He probably lives in the Mission."

"The *Avenues*," Nicholas said.

"Richmond," Nicholas said.

"Dance with me," my brother said.

He pulled me from my chair with a strength that I gave in to. He pulled me to the dance floor, to the center of it. He put my hands on his waist. He put his arms around my neck, blew soft, liquored air on my face, and began to take small steps, moving in place, to no music that was being played in that room.

"Dance with me," he said.

He wrapped his hair around my neck and pulled me to him with it. He moved his hands down my back, pressed me closer to him, and he pressed hard to me.

Our clothes touched everywhere.

"Why don't you *dance* with me!"

I clasped my hands around his waist, practically encircling it. I let my hands become the accessory he wanted.

He made his eyes look as if they were looking into mine.

"Dance with me," he said.

I danced with him.

We left the man from San Francisco with the most beautiful men in Rome. We walked back to the hotel and said very little for most of the walk.

"Just one thing," I finally said. "The Empress of China wasn't there when you were twelve."

"Actually, it wasn't the Empress of China," my brother said. "It was the place that was there *before* it was the Empress of China."

"Chinese?"

"Of course Chinese. We had cashew chicken."

"What was a Japanese man doing there?"

"It *is* a little odd, isn't it?"

"A Jap in a Chink joint?" I asked.

Nicholas considered this. "As it were," he said, "if you will. I don't know what he was doing there. I mean, actually, sweetheart, I didn't ask him, 'So, what's a nice Jap like you doing in a Chink joint like this?' It did not exactly cross my mind to ask him that. Maybe he liked cashew chicken. Maybe he had a yen for sweet and sour. How would I know what he was doing there?"

We walked a block.

"Just one other thing," I said. "Why would Mother leave you, when you were twelve years old, at a bar at three in the afternoon?"

"I said why. Didn't I say that she had to run an errand?"

"What errand would make a woman leave a twelve-year-old boy at the bar of a Chink joint at three in the afternoon?"

"Honey, what's this Chink business? What's all this business about Japs and Chinks and Japs in Chink joints? Who have you been seeing lately, honey?"

We crossed the street and walked to the end of the next block, to the hotel entrance. We had to ring to get in. Nicholas lit a cigarette while we waited.

"She had to dash to Gump's," he said. "She had her eye on some jade ashtrays at Gump's."

I have made up my mind that it must be Chichén Itzá. Even though it had almost nothing for sale, Chichén Itzá was another of Nicholas's favorite places in the world. He went there more than once; there were a few years, I think, when he went there every year. The skull faces behind him in the photograph, if I am not mistaken, are the ones that run along the walls of the ruins of the ball court. The faces run in rows and have long teeth. They do not smile, either.

Nicholas and I went to Chichén Itzá once, and it occurred to me that I might even have taken the photograph, years ago, until I realized that I had not before seen my brother in this particular Japanese robe.

I am wondering how, exactly, he got to the ruins in the Japanese robe. The hotel in Chichén Itzá, the one where Nicholas would have stayed when he went back without me, the one where peacocks run loose in the gardens, devouring papayas that the clientele toss down from balconies, is about half a mile from the site. One can walk to the ruins on the shoulder of the road, and I am wondering if that is what Nicholas did. On the shoulder of the road that one takes to the ruins in Chichén Itzá, as on many roads in

Mexico, one will see, frequently, a horse or a cow that has been hit, burning. One sees the animal in flames. On many roads in Mexico, when a horse or a cow is hit, the natives ignite it with gasoline. Sometimes the animal is alive when it is ignited, and one can see, from one's car, or on foot if one is walking, the animal dying of the impact while it is dying also of the fire. One sees the animal convulse. The smell of the fire and the flesh is also a taste. It gets into the throat, the carcass taste, with the smell of smoke and the taste of blood in the swallow of each breath.

Of course, Nicholas may not have walked. He may have gone by car, but I can picture my brother on foot, tight-waisted in the Japanese robe, passing an animal on fire in a ditch. I can picture the flow of the robe, the lilt in my brother's walk, unbroken by the stench, and it occurs to me that, in his mind, Nicholas may already have been planning the composition of the photograph.

Nicholas liked to refer to photographs of himself as *shots*. it was his word to distinguish photographs of himself from photographs in general. On occasions when Nicholas and I were photographed together, which became rare, Nicholas would say, "This is a good photograph of you, but it is not a becoming shot of me."

On his way to the ruins, Nicholas may have known, even then, that he would enlarge the photograph of himself, the one for which he may have walked around a burning animal to pose, and that he would hang it on a mirrored wall, within a mirrored frame, in exact proportion to the size of life.

He may have decided in advance that it would be a stunning shot.

The year that Nicholas and I went to Chichén Itzá was the year we sold the house we had grown up in. It was four years after the summer in Madrid, not quite a year after the time in Rome when he swam in the Tiber. It was the year that Nicholas left California and moved east, and a year or so before he went back with another man to Chichén Itzá and posed in the Japanese robe, in front of the skull faces, for the life-size photograph.

Or rather, the life-size *shot*.

We spent three nights at the hotel with the peacocks, a long stay for Chichén Itzá, but we stayed because Nicholas decided that Spanish was the most beautiful language in the world when he heard a bus boy say good morning. When I pointed out that the bus boy had said good morning in English, Nicholas said that was not the point.

"When he says just 'good morning' in English, I hear something else in Spanish," Nicholas said. "I hear epithalamia."

"Epithalamiums," I said.

"What?"

"Epithalamiums. The plural of epithalamium is epithalamiums. You hear epithalamiums."

Nicholas smiled with one lip. "Now, darling," he said, "let's don't get carried away. How many of them do you think I hear?"

We could, of course, have heard Spanish any-where, but that, too, I suppose, was not the point. Nicholas wanted to hear the bus boy's Spanish, though that year, I think, was about the time, roughly, that Nicholas began to narrow his range to exclude bus boys. That year, I think, Nicholas would not have bothered to tell giants in crew cuts to fuck Mom. That year, in the afternoons, after visits to the ruins — visits which did not, until the third day, include the climb up the pyramid, because he was afraid of the climb down — my brother played chess by the pool of the hotel in Chichén Itzá with a man who turned out to be from New York and who had, inside an unbuttoned, short-sleeved madras shirt, a covering of white hair across his chest.

On trips, my brother increasingly met men of a certain age who turned out to be from New York. He would play chess with them, though Nicholas was not, in any sense, a player of the game. None of the men ever seemed to mind when Nicholas asked, as he always did, why the game had to go on after the capture of his queen.

"I mean," Nicholas always asked, "isn't that more or less *it*?"

The year in Chichén Itzá, the last trip we took together, when he saw the man with white chest hair by the pool, Nicholas came over from his chaise and sat on my towel.

I could smell his suntan cream because I used oil. Even his skin was different. There was nothing about him that I thought was the same.

Nicholas began to rub my back. But what he gave me was not a backrub. He moved up with his hands from the waistband of my trunks and came around under my arms, until I felt his fingers pulling at my hairs in front.

My brother lowered his lips to my ear.

He whispered, "You could throw that down in front of a fire and have a symposium on it. You could do *frottage*."

To "have a symposium" was one of my brother's several euphemisms for bed. Nicholas never called things by their names if he could call them something else. He was saying that the man's white chest hair was the proverbial fur rug.

I felt my brother's fingers. I felt his breath in my ear.

He whispered, "Do you think it's a merkin?"

Merkin was one of my brother's favorite words that year. It was the year of merkin and *frottage*. We had been through the years of *panache*, of *faux pas*, of *de trop*.

I answered that I did not think it was a merkin. I suggested that no one would be apt to wear a white merkin.

"You're right," my brother whispered. He pulled a hair out from my front and laughed when I winced.

"When you're as old as he is," Nicholas whispered, "I want you to dye these merkins. I want you to do that for me. I want you to promise now to dye these merkins for Big Mama."

Nicholas sometimes called himself Big Mama. I think it was his way to remind me that he was the one who was the child.

"Promise Big Mama," my brother whispered that afternoon in front of the man in the open madras shirt.

"Promise Big Mama *now*."

Nicholas waited until the third day to climb the pyramid. It was the prospect of a photograph, I think, that got him to the top. I told him that I would take his picture up there, with all the view around him.

"Never mind the view," he said. "Skip the view."

The steps up are steep and look steeper going down. Halfway up, Nicholas looked behind him, down, and I saw panic in his face. He said I had better make him look his best, because it might be the last time anyone would see him in one piece. He said that he was sure that he would never get down. He said that I must do him justice, make him look divine, because that was what he would probably need to be.

"Take it like a lover would," he told me at the top.

That year, my brother could actually sit on his hair. His ribs pressed ridges out against his shirt. He faced away from me, looking down at the ruins. As I began to focus on his back, Nicholas turned around, pressed his hair against his ribs, and casually upstaged a circle of horizon.

He touched a cheekbone and ran a finger down along his jawline, testing the edge. This was a ritual that Nicholas went through before a photograph. He also went through it in front of mirrors. In Chichén Itzá, I had seen him go through it every morning, before he scrubbed his face with rough towels that he saturated in tequila for astringent.

In Italy he used grappa; in France he used framboise.

On days that the cheekbones or the jawline did not feel to the touch as he thought they should, days he called his harridan days, days he called himself a termagant, Nicholas, wherever we were, would find an issue of *Time* or *Newsweek* and would turn at once to "Milestones" or "Transition." He would read in silence, until he made his choice. Then I would learn the death of the week most salient to Nicholas.

"God help me," he would say. "I look like Helena Rubinstein."

Or it would be, "God help me, I look like Linda Darnell."

On trips with my brother, I heard in this way of many illustrious passings, even on weeks when no one illustrious had passed.

Nicholas always said that the best people died when one was traveling, but there were weeks of disappointing milestones, dismal transitions, passings which were, for Nicholas, deficient. On such weeks, my brother would assign untimely demise to names that came to mind.

"God help me," he would say. "I look like Miriam Hopkins."

"God help me, I look like Clare Boothe Luce."

"God help me, I look like Olive Higgins Prouty."

Sometimes I would find a name a shock and would ask Nicholas if it was true, if the one he had named was really dead in Transition.

Nicholas would answer without looking up. "Not yet, but can you imagine how she must *look*?"

But that afternoon on the pyramid, the chee' bones and the jawline must have pleased my br^n- er's fingers. He must have believed that he l^ed more glamorous than a transition. He must l^e be- lieved that his face was in order.

His face was in order.

I waited while my brother shook his hair out, to give it volume for the photograph.

His hair did not need volume, his hair had volume.

But he kept shaking it.

Bent over, with his hair sweeping the top of the pyramid, Nicholas turned his head away.

"Do you know the difference," he asked, "between beauty of the spirit and beauty that is merely physical?"

I knew that I could not give him the answer that he seemed impatient to give back. I asked him the difference.

"Physical," Nicholas said, "the kind of beauty that is merely physical, is the kind that can't be faked. In other words, inner beauty is what counts, but outer beauty is what *shows.*"

As I watched my brother paying tribute to his hair, while I thought over his remark, it occurred to me that I had probably never witnessed, even from Nicholas, an exhibit of so much self-regard accompanied by so much deserving.

I was about to take the picture when a half-dead-looking dog appeared in the frame. The dog sniffed n brother's feet.

hen Nicholas saw the dog, he waved his hand in t of his face to stop the picture. He knelt down on t tone. He said, "Poochie."

He looked up at me. "This is a very old poochie-boy. No, this is a very old poochie-*girl*. Look at this beast, look at this darling old beast."

I replied that I did not want to look at the beast, that the beast was putrescent.

The dog was everything that a dog should not be. It looked too old to be alive, emaciated, flabby at the same time, and its stringy coat was patched with dried-on mud. I did not understand how Nicholas could get as close as he was to anything that looked the way the creature did. I had seen my brother shield his face in Mexican markets to block out slightly over-ripe papayas. Ordinarily, he was revolted by men in short-sleeved shirts; he had a horror of clip-on bow ties. Yet there he was, kneeling down beside the creature on the stone.

It had not occurred to me to tell him not to touch the animal, until I saw my brother's fingers slide into the filthy coat.

He rubbed the dog between its ribs, then down inside the cavity of its belly. Something that looked like gentleness showed in his fingers, and I heard my brother murmur to the dog, though I could not hear the words that he murmured.

His murmuring had the same gentleness that I had heard or actually, not heard, not exactly, when I had seen my brother murmur to babies in carriages. That was a thing my brother did. In parks, in stores, on sidewalks, Nicholas murmured to babies. The murmurs, I think, were not meant to be heard, though I suspect that Nicholas did intend to be seen murmuring.

When Nicholas murmured to babies, as when he murmured to animals, the same look came over his face. It was an expression that could be mistaken for a smile, and as I watched him with the dog, it crossed my mind that if I were willing to risk the outburst, the tantrum, then the pique and frosty silence that would follow, I had, just then, the closest opportunity that I was ever likely to get to take a picture of my brother smiling.

But it would not have been worth the tantrum and the frost. The few times that I had caught Nicholas unposed, he had found the camera and destroyed the film. Nicholas would crack the combination on my suitcase to get at film he wanted to destroy.

"Look at it," Nicholas said. "This is an *ancient* beast. How do you think it got up here?"

I offered that perhaps its owner had carried it up and left it. I offered this even though the creature was clearly an animal that no one owned. I said that the Mayans had sacrificed virgins, that this, perhaps, was a sacrificial dog.

"That is not funny," Nicholas said. "For saying that, you can carry it down."

I said that nothing could make me carry the dog

down, that nothing could make me touch it. I told Nicholas that the dog probably had every Mexican dog disease that there was in the world.

Nicholas knew how to do something with his eyes, and he did it then. It was a trick he had that made him appear to be on the verge of tears. He could stay on the verge of tears for hours, with the trick.

It was not the trick that actually did produce tears, though Nicholas had that trick, too. That was another trick, one he had not used on me for several years.

"Someone has to take it down," Nicholas said. "It will never get down by itself."

There were a few other people on the top that afternoon, a few men other than myself who looked able to carry a dog down a pyramid. Nicholas approached each one of them, and each man looked at the dog, then at Nicholas, and even when my brother offered money, each man shook his head, refused, walked off.

Nicholas went to the edge of the pyramid and sat on the top step, on his hair, with the dog. I could tell that he was looking down the steps.

With all that there was to look at from where I stood — the ancient structures of the site, the landscape stretching out in flatness to horizons that kept going — what I looked at, until he turned around, was my brother sitting on his hair. I looked at his back, his straight chain of spine, the ribs that were ridges in his shirt, and the childlike arms, slight within the sleeves that were buttoned at the wrist.

When he turned around, I saw a single tear poised halfway down my brother's face.

That tear was teardrop shaped.

It was the perfect tear for Nicholas.

He said, "Get this creature out of my shot."

The number of steps up the pyramid in Chichén Itzá is three hundred and sixty-five. It is also the number down. I know this because Nicholas told me while we were descending. Nicholas took each step slowly, sitting briefly on each one before pushing off with his hands, lowering himself to the next.

He looked down with each push on the grade of the descent. He recited what he knew, things that came to mind, as if he believed, or wanted to believe, that random facts could get him to the ground.

All the way down, he recited. Most of what I know about Chichén Itzá is what I remember my brother telling me, while I came down, on foot, beside him. I have no idea if what he said is true.

I stayed with him step by step, because he asked me to.

Nicholas told me that the builders of the pyramid had known their calendar to be inexact. He told me that Mayan calculations of the sun had differed from ours by seventeen seconds per year. He told me that the pyramid, the one we were descending, had been built up from the base of a pyramid built before. The inner pyramid had been discovered, Nicholas said, during excavation of the pyramid that could be seen. A temple was found, and because the inner pyramid had been covered for centuries, the treasures of its temple were intact.

Halfway down, Nicholas mentioned other ruins on the site and said that structures within structures were everywhere around us. Chichén Itzá had been built, he said, upon a conquered site, by conquerers who had themselves been conquered in another place. They had lost their city, and when they set about to duplicate, in a new place, the city they had lost, they built outward from the mass of the structures they had conquered.

The inner pyramid contained, my brother said, evidence of customs not known about before. Pieces of jade, he told me, were placed on the tongues of the dead. It had been believed, he said, that jade in the mouth assured food after life.

When we were near the bottom of the pyramid, near the ground, Nicholas told me that in funerary ceremonies, objects of sacrifice were painted red. It was a color, Nicholas explained, close to cinnabar or even *sang de boeuf*, and when the tomb was sealed its doors were also sealed in that red.

When we reached the ground, I was thinking about

the calendar. I was wondering about the seventeen seconds and whether the Mayan year had been longer by that much, or shorter, than the year that we now take to be true.

This was the question that I asked my brother on the ground.

Nicholas looked up at the pyramid.

"Honey," he said, "are you sure you got that creature out?"

It has been a while, but as I recall, they were horses, for the most part, they were not cows, the animals that Nicholas and I saw burning in the ditches off the roads.

It was the thought of my brother walking to the ruins to be photographed in the robe that made me wonder, while I was filling the champagne glass with the last of the tequila, which it would have been that Nicholas might have had to pass, a burning horse or a burning cow.

I am in the doorway with the glass, and as I look into the room at the photograph, I realize that it would have been neither horse nor cow, because it comes to me that it was not in Chichén Itzá that we saw the animals on fire.

I was wrong.

We saw the animals on fire in the mountains, outside Acapulco on the way to Cuernavaca. We saw the animals on fire years before we ever went to Chichén Itzá. We were with our mother and our father when we saw the animals on fire.

I remember our father telling me to cover my brother's eyes.

I remember covering them.

I sit on the bed with the glass. I settle on the cashmere blanket. The cigarette burn in it fits around my finger like a ring.

I am wondering how Nicholas could sleep in this room.

In the mirrored frame, under the glass, even the photograph of my brother becomes a mirror.

In the same mirrored frame, on the same mirrored wall, I cannot say which one of us, my brother or myself, would keep me more awake.

The mirrors make me wonder how Nicholas felt when he looked at himself. I wonder if Nicholas really believed that cheekbones have bad days. I wonder to what extent, exactly, a slack jawline could make him feel like a milestone or a transition.

Then I catch my own face in the lacquer.

God help me, I look like Edith Head.

Earlier today, before I came into these rooms, I picked up the keys from the woman who called me two days ago in California to tell me about Nicholas. The night before she called me, Nicholas had not shown up at the woman's house for dinner. It was like him, the woman explained, to appear an hour late, but not like him to not appear at all. Over the telephone, I did not tell the woman that she did not need to tell me what was and was not like him. When he did not answer his telephone that night or the next day, the woman let herself in with the keys that Nicholas had left with her, so that he would always have a spare, so that the woman could check his mail and look after his jade trees and use his garden, if she wanted, when he was away. The woman explained that for years Nicholas had had a man come to the house to look after the garden, the jade trees, the plants on the roof, but that he did not trust the man to be in the house when he was away. The woman explained all this — why she happened to have keys — and said that when she let herself in with the keys she happened to have, she found my brother on his bed with contusions on his neck.

She called me from his phone, the one in the study with the automatic dial. She introduced herself, said she was in my brother's study — though she called it a den — sitting at his desk. She told me she had just then pushed the button labeled "brotherkins."

I was surprised that Nicholas had me on his automatic dial. As I learned today, most of the buttons on this telephone are marked with names of restaurants.

The woman lives several blocks west of here, in a fifth-floor walkup on Horatio Street. She took me, when I arrived, into a small, orderly kitchen, where she was cooking a hot dog for a four-year-old boy. Some lentils were soaking on a counter in a pot. I supposed they were soaking for soup. She was a hefty, unfashionable woman — an unlikely friend, I thought, for Nicholas to have.

The woman turned the hot dog, said she would be with me in a minute. Then, quietly, in other words than these, she asked me not to refer to my brother by name in front of her little boy.

She chose her words to talk around what the boy could understand, but I put it together that my brother had been, of all things, the little boy's godfather, that the little boy had adored him and had taken it hard when told of his death.

The woman told the little boy to wash his hands for lunch. When he was out of the room she said she didn't know why she had told him when she did, that she could have waited, but it had seemed to her to be a time when the best thing to do with the truth is get it over with, get it behind you the first chance that you get, because it is not a thing that will turn out better later.

The little boy came back, showed his hands to me. He seemed all right. It was the woman who didn't.

I tried to imagine my brother and this woman as friends. I tried to imagine Nicholas being friends with a woman who calls a study a den. I could imagine neither thing, nor could I imagine my brother as any child's godfather. When I could imagine nothing else, though I do not cook and am in no way partial to lentil soup, it came to me all at once to ask the woman for her recipe.

The woman gave me a look from the stove. She said nothing. I watched her fork the hot dog from the pan, put it on a plate, and cut it into bite-sized pieces. She put mustard on the pieces and set the plate down in front of the boy.

The woman apologized that she had nothing to offer me except some vermouth. At the same time, the little boy said that he did not want mustard, he wanted ketchup. The woman took his plate to the sink, wiped off the mustard with a paper towel, and pounded ketchup from a bottle onto the pieces, for the boy.

Then she said that she was wrong, she had forgotten, there wasn't only vermouth, that my brother had brought over some tequila the last time he'd come for dinner, two weeks or so before. It was still half there, the woman said.

I took the vermouth.

The woman took some, too, and we left the child at the table and went into the next room. The couch was sectional. We sat down with our glasses, and that was when the woman, in no context to speak of, told me that for the past several years, years I did not see him, Nicholas had taken to carrying photographs of himself in his wallet, photographs from ten or more years before, five or six different poses at a time and always changing — Nicholas in Cuernavaca, Nicholas in Taxco, Nicholas in Rome, on a stage where one year we heard *Turandot* performed at the Baths of Caracalla; Nicholas tan, Nicholas thin, looking the way he was supposed to look, the way he did when he still looked like himself.

The woman told me that on more than one occasion, after dinner and some drinks, Nicholas would take the photographs from his wallet, show them to her, that he would say, "This is how the face looked in 1968."

"Not 'this is how *I* looked,'" the woman told me. "What he said every time was 'this is how *the face* looked.'"

It was along these same lines, more or less, that the woman told me of a time, just a few months ago, when she and Nicholas had taken the little boy to Coney Island. It was not easy to imagine Nicholas at Coney Island, so I did not put myself to the trouble. The woman told me that shortly after that excursion she showed my brother some photographs, casual snapshots, from that Coney Island day.

When my brother saw these photographs, the woman told me, he went at them at once with a ball-point.

She then showed me the photographs, so I saw for myself where my brother had inked in an indentation to slenderize his waist, where he had carved blue hollows into his face to put cheekbones on his cheeks.

The woman told me that my brother had re-contoured twenty-eight of thirty-six exposures, without speaking, for well over an hour.

"As you can see," the woman said, "he did it quite artistically."

I could see how he had done it.

The woman told me that after he had finished with the photographs, Nicholas gave them back and helped her put the little boy to bed. She told me that the little boy adored my brother's bedtime stories. That night, the night he carved ball-point hollows into his face, the story that he told the little boy began — the woman remembered — "There was a little boy who lived in a shoe. He had so many clothes he didn't know what to do."

"Except," the woman said, "I think he said *frocks*."

I said yes, that he probably would have said frocks.

Then the woman gave us more vermouth and told me step by step how to make lentil soup.

When he was little, one of our grandmothers told Nicholas that little boys who stare at themselves too much in mirrors grow up to be ugly men.

Nicholas asked if the same thing was true for little girls.

Our grandmother told him it was not.

"Then why," my brother asked, "are there so many ugly women?"

I reminded Nicholas of this the morning of the day that we saw the dog on the pyramid.

From my bed, I could see my brother in the bathroom mirror. Nicholas always kept the door open while he scrubbed his face, as if each inspection of his cheekbones should be viewed as an event.

In the same mirror, I could see myself in bed as I watched him.

I looked at my brother in the mirror and repeated what our grandmother, years ago, had told him.

It was to the mirror that my brother answered back.

"Lamb chop," he said, "I have been staring at myself my whole life, and I'm not ugly yet."

He kept scrubbing his face.

"Anyway," Nicholas said, "there is one thing you can always say back to the dead about the claims they made. You can always say, 'Honey, look who's dead, and look at who's alive.'"

The night of the day that we saw the dog on the pyramid, Nicholas insisted on inviting the man in the short-sleeved madras shirt to join us for dinner. The man, thank God, did not wear the madras shirt. He wore French cuffs — a tad *de trop* for Chichén Itzá.

Nicholas made a show of being annoyed by the man's attentions to the bus boy.

"Trust me," Nicholas told the man. "You don't want anything to do with that one. That one has been around. That one is not exactly a pristine commodity. All the perfumes of Siberia could not get that one clean."

The man gave me a wink. It was not his first wink of the night. "He's jealous," the man said to me. "He loves me already."

"You're sweet," my brother said to the man. "But you are ancient enough to be my father."

The man said, "I'm a father figure."

"I've had a father figure," Nicholas said. "My father was a father figure. But you are also old enough to be my Sugar Daddy. Are you *rich* enough to be my Sugar Daddy?"

"Is he drunk?" the man asked. The man had an irritating habit of speaking to Nicholas through me.

Nicholas said, "I am not drunk. How rich are you?"

Nicholas never knew when he was drunk. When he was drunk, Nicholas thought he was captivating.

The man smiled at my brother, a broad, slap-on-the-back kind of smile.

"Yes, I can see them," Nicholas said. "Handsome, costly looking teeth. But tell me in *numbers*. How much mon-mon do you have?"

"What does the boy want?" the man asked me.

"I think he wants to know how much mon-mon you have," I said.

"Doesn't it break your heart," the man asked me, "that something that looks like this *is* like this?"

The man winked at me again.

Nicholas put his hand on the man's arm and smiled back at him. It was all bright teeth between them at the table.

"Nice cuff links," my brother told the man. "I'm mad for ostentation."

My brother played his fingers on the cuff links. There were small diamonds in them. Nicholas covered the diamonds with his fingers. He made his fingers look musical.

"I *dote* on ostentation," Nicholas said. "Tell me numbers."

"Is he like this all the time?" the man asked me.

Nicholas pulled his hand back. "You're not going to tell me how rich you are?"

The man smiled at my brother in a way I found obscene.

"It is a shame," Nicholas said, after a bit. "I love Chichén Itzá, but you can never get a decent dinner here. They have never heard of cooking here. Look at these Mexican *pommes frites.*"

Nicholas held up a strip of fried potato, examined it. He took a small bite, made a critical face, then deposited what was left of the potato onto the edge of the man's plate.

"These Mexican *pommes frites* can go to hell," my brother said to the man.

He dropped his napkin on the table. Then he left the table. He slipped through narrow spaces between other tables, moving toward the bar. At the end of the bar, he turned a corner, disappeared. As exits go, it had played well; the man with the cuff links had watched it. Everyone had watched it.

"You don't look a lot alike," the man said to me when Nicholas was gone.

I must have said something.

"It's an act, isn't it?" the man asked me. "The brother bit? The pretty one likes to pretend, so you keep him happy, you go along with it. Am I right?"

I must have said nothing.

The man leaned forward. I watched his hands slide across the table, toward mine. Without my brother's fingers over them, the diamond cuff links did not look like much.

The man touched my hand.

"I'm right," he said.

Across the street, where the mannequins stay lighted through the night, young men gather, late, to lean against the glass. Dressed for summer, for conquest, fit, tanned, gleaming, they share the street with the sculpted figures on display. They arrange themselves, these living specimens of youth, and each one lets the light strike his premium places. Once the young men find the light that suits them, they do not move, they rarely even shift, and all down the block, window after window, the street would be in stillness, if it were not for the reasons that they come, each one of them, with the insolence that is the other side of yearning.

Others come — paler, older, strolling. Some stroll dogs on leashes, others offer cigarettes when they stop to chat.

Eventually, the young and old pair off.

This, also, is what my brother could look out on every night. I would not live over this.

I do not know the going rate for youth today. I never have known. The closest that I came to knowing was when Nicholas took in what he referred to as his chess winnings. For about ten years, until the end of his twenties, Nicholas referred to the cigarette cases, the clothes, the paintings, all that he was given by men, as his winnings.

"Look at my new frock," my brother would say, his voice up an octave with delight.

"Look at my new *bibelot*."

Gimcrack.

Cadeau.

Objet pas exactement trouvé.

One year, from one man, Nicholas acquired items of malachite. From another, he became a collector of netsukes. The Japanese robes, if I am right, were gifts from more than one man. When I asked him, once, how he felt, taking money from men, Nicholas insisted that he did not take money from men, he took presents from men.

I suggested that taking netsukes instead of money did not make him less a catamite. For a minute, I thought Nicholas was offended by the word. I watched him turn a netsuke over in his palm. It was ivory, an insect on bamboo, with black coral eyes inlaid. Nicholas turned it over more than once, holding it at different angles, as if it were vital to choose the most becoming, and when he looked at me, his face made me wish that I had said anything else.

"Don't you think you're being a trifle *technical?*" he said.

I replied that I had not intended to be technical.

"Let's don't linger over it," he said.

I saw in my brother's narrowed eyes that he could read my thoughts and never miss. He could make me embarrassed, ashamed, because he, unmistakably, was not. I was convinced that Nicholas could read the grammar of a thoughtwave.

"This is a dragonfly at rest on bamboo," he said. "Notice how the ivory simulates the grain of bamboo."

Nicholas held the netsuke to the light for me to see. I could see the simulated grain, but I wondered, and I asked, why the artist had not *used* bamboo.

Nicholas overlooked my question with an eyebrow. "Did you know," he asked, "that dragonflies are so light, so weightless, that they can stay in the air with perfect stillness?"

It occurred to me that Nicholas must have meant this information to mean something.

My brother took up another netsuke. "This one," he said, "is a cicada emerging from its chrysalis. Its wings are carved from tortoise. Look how my finger shows through it. Did you know that a cicada lives ten years in its chrysalis, feeding underground on the sap of roots?"

I did not find it necessary to say I had not known this.

"And this one," he said, showing me yet another netsuke, yet another present from a man. "This one is a mask, an exact miniature of what the lead actor wears on stage. Notice this," he said, and slowly turned and angled the mask. "Now notice this." He turned it again, to another angle, then slowly to another. At the different angles, the small carved mask in my brother's hand took on different expressions — anger, scheming, grief, remorse.

In my brother's hand, the mask changed face.

"That is what the actors do," my brother said. "They get every expression, convey every emotion, just by turning their heads, like this, like that. They play their part, their whole character that way, just by turning the mask. That's their whole performance, just the angling of the mask. The mask stays the same, of course. It is the same mask throughout the play, it is only the angles that change."

The mask, he said, was carved from lacquer, from thousands of layers of lacquer. He told me of the skill required to carve such detail into so brittle a material. He told me to imagine the patience.

"Actually, there is a difference," Nicholas said, "between taking presents and taking money. It is the difference between a tribute and a transaction."

I expect that Nicholas did believe this.

"I never take anything that does not delight me," he said. "I never take things from more than one man at a time, and I never take anything that I could not buy myself."

I expect that Nicholas believed that these were points of honor.

I am even inclined to believe that he meant it when he said, "There is nothing wrong with Sugar Daddies, *per se*. Sugar Daddies are only tawdry when one needs them."

I took notice of the words.

Apparently, we had come to the year of *per se*.

The photograph of my brother in the Japanese robe may have been taken by the man in Chichén Itzá, not the year that we were there, but later, a year they may have gone back together. The man in Chichén Itzá was one of the men Nicholas knew for a while.

The diamond cuff links are here, in this room, in a box.

I think the man in Chichén Itzá was the malachite man. I do not think he was the netsuke man.

I did not lose track of the men; I never kept track. It was not that there were so many, but I tried not to hear about them. This was not difficult, until the last one, the one who left Nicholas, rather than the other way around. Until the one who left him, whom I heard about then, I heard more about the presents than about the men who gave them.

The man who left my brother was the one who gave him the lacquer table. I know this because the year that the man left him, Nicholas offered to sell me the lacquer table at what he called a "nothing" price. The figure that he named was not a "nothing" figure.

The night that Nicholas tried to sell me the lacquer table, the night I heard about the man, we were having dinner at what had been our father's club, a place we had often been to as children, a club to which I still belong. This was the night that I watched Nicholas devour four triple lamb chops. Two years before, I had seen him order shrimp and only suck the shells. In Rome, I had seen him move a fork around a plate of *porcini* and never take a bite. But at our father's club, Nicholas gnawed bones and told me, in detail, the history of the lacquering technique.

He told me about the monks in Japan. I gathered that Nicholas did research on his winnings.

He also told me that when the man gave him the lacquer table, he, in turn, gave the man, for his forty-seventh birthday, forty-seven presents.

Nicholas described each one of the forty-seven presents. "I thought that it was time," he said, "to try out reciprocity."

My brother told me that when the man left him, he used to look for the man's car on streets outside the all-night bars. Nicholas had never been in one of those bars, he told me, until he went looking for the man. I did not know why Nicholas was telling me this, and I did not know why he wanted me to buy the lacquer table. He wanted me to buy the lacquer table, he said, with the understanding that he could buy it back from me, for the same price, if he changed his mind.

Nicholas used the word *proviso*.

When I told him that I saw, in these terms, no advantage for me, Nicholas waved his hand in front of his face.

"Let's skip it," he said.

I was willing to do just that, and then a waiter brought my brother's second plate of lamb chops.

Nicholas cut into the flesh.

"I cannot imagine," he said, "how anyone could get tired of *me*."

When I said nothing, Nicholas said, "I mean, I find it *unimaginable.*"

Nicholas went on about how unimaginable he found it.

I drank a B&B and watched my brother eat. I was baffled by his greed for food, but I wondered even more about his lust to sell a present. He claimed that he had never sold a present, and I was inclined to believe that he had not.

I thought about presents, I thought about money. Tributes and transactions.

When my brother was thirteen, he asked our mother if my bones had stopped growing, and when our mother told him that they had, Nicholas bought me a gold ring. It was, he told me at the time, technically, a wedding ring for a man, and inside it, all around the band, Nicholas had ordered an inscription. There are reasons that I have not worn the ring, and until two days ago, I had not looked at it for more than twenty years. But I have carried the inscription in my mind. Nicholas had the ring inscribed in Hebrew, a language he did not know. The inscription is not a line from the Old Testament; it is from no Hebrew source. It is a sentence Nicholas made up and had translated. He could have chosen Greek, he could have chosen Japanese, but Nicholas chose Hebrew. I did not ask why, because the year Nicholas gave me the ring was the year that Elizabeth Taylor had become a Jew.

Nicholas told me that he had paid for the ring by dressing up poor and singing on streets. It is possible, though not very, that he did this. At the time I wondered, what, exactly, Nicholas would have chosen to dress up in to look poor. If he dressed up poor, if he sang on streets, it was not in order to pay for the ring. Nicholas paid for the ring with money that he took from our father's armoire, from a drawer that was supposed to be secret. I know this, because when our father noticed the loss, our father, then well into his sixties, called me in to his dressing room to ask me what to do about a thirteen-year-old boy.

I told our father to let it go.

Nicholas must have known that our father would let it go. I was impressed by my brother for finding the hidden drawer and taking the money. I was impressed, too, by his apparent notion of himself as unpunishable. I used to look in our father's armoire, in the drawers, under the shirts, alert at all times to the risk of being caught. Nicholas, I expect, did not think in terms of risk.

Our father's dressing room had chairs, tables, ashtrays. You could sit in the wing chair in our father's dressing room and smoke a cigarette; when I was a boy it was the place I went to smoke.

My brother was the only one who found me. He would appear in the doorway, posed with his hand out, and command, "Give me a lovely cigarette."

Nicholas never asked for just a puff.

Under the shirts in his drawers, our father kept magazines which in those years I thought I should want to look at. Smoking with my brother, I would point to a female chest.

I would say something like, look at these.

"What about them?" Nicholas would ask me, puffing.

"Tell Mama the truth," I heard my brother say seven years ago to a young man sitting on a pool table in an all-night bar. "What would you say if I told you that you were my type, tonight?"

Nicholas had taken me to a place where men did not wear ties. Ties were not allowed. Sweaters were not allowed. The sign at the door listed what was not allowed. Cologne was not allowed. Certain kinds of shirts were not allowed. Shirts could be checked at the door. Anything could be checked at the door. Some men checked everything but their shoes.

The pool table was not used for pool.

I was surprised that Nicholas would bring me to the kind of place it was. I was surprised, too, by his attention to the young man on the pool table.

The young man was younger than Nicholas.

That year Nicholas was thirty years old.

At the bar, tickets were exchanged for drinks. The bar was not licensed to sell liquor, but it was legal to sell tickets. The liquor was house brands and was served in plastic glasses. Most everyone drank beer from cans.

Nicholas did not drink beer from cans.

"Take that right back to the place where you got it," Nicholas said when I brought him a can. "Mama does not drink *suds*. Mama especially does not drink suds from *containers*. Mama will drink her bourbon in her *Styrofoam*."

Nicholas drank bourbon in what Nicholas called Styrofoam. It was in fact clear plastic, and the sight of my brother drinking bourbon from a plastic glass struck me, that night, as close to the most unlikely thing that I had seen him do. That night seven years ago when he was thirty years old was the last night I saw my brother.

I cannot remember what the young man on the pool table answered. The young man on the pool table wore no shirt. He wore the kind of trousers that young men like him wore, a kind that was allowed.

"Maybe you can tell me," Nicholas said, "why everybody wears these trousers, with the labels in the back that tell the waist size. Why do all of you want to go around telling the world your waist size? I mean, *disclosing* it. And maybe you can tell me why it is always, always thirty."

If the young man said anything memorable, I do not remember it.

"Of course, I can understand the buttons in the front," Nicholas told the young man. "Everyone knows that they are quieter in movie theaters. But what is the point of broadcasting your waist size on your backside? I mean, *exposing* it. Why does everybody in the world want to do this?"

The young man indolently asked my brother his waist size.

Of course, it was only Nicholas who could ask anything he wanted. He turned to me and said that we should take a tour of the back.

He said, "Let's *promener*."

"*Se promener*," I said.

"Okay, let's *se promener*," he said.

The narrow rooms in back aspired to the spirit of a blackout at the "Y." Bare, low-watt bulbs led down to darker basement rooms, fervid with the smell of nitrites.

"It's an *oubliette*," Nicholas whispered to me in the dark.

It occurred to me that he could have also called it the new light for bone structure.

Every step meant a brush with flesh.

In a corner, a throng of men circled a group of three. The throng, in frenzy as one body, snapped and hissed instructions to the men inside, detailed orders, graphic and insistent, with which the three men within the circle, moaning, more or less complied.

One of the three men began to roar, then another, then the third. The men surrounding them roared too, broke out in gaudy tribute.

Then I heard my brother's voice rise over them.

"Oh, come on, boys," he shrieked. "It doesn't feel *that* good!"

I was certain that his inflection had been practiced.

Perhaps two men laughed. But the throng, which had had one thing on its mind, was about to get another. The silence was public, a room making up its mind. For a time that was not going to last, the room was so quiet you could have heard a person die.

Before anyone could get to him, I pulled my brother from the crowd, to a fire exit near the stairs.

On the street, I pressed him up against the fire door. I shouted at him that it was not a good idea to sneer at men having public sex. I shouted that men having public sex were not famous for their collective sense of humor.

Nicholas gave me a weary look. "Honey, that's all right. You're being humorous enough for everyone."

I kept shouting at him. Nicholas tried to shake out of my hold.

"May we break this pose, please?" he asked. "You're getting my face wet."

I let him go. I backed off.

Nicholas wiped his face with his sleeve.

"Do you want to get your shirt?" my brother asked me.

I had been wearing a kind of shirt that had not been allowed. It had occurred to me that Nicholas must have known that I would be made to check it. Nicholas, of course, had worn nothing that he had been made to check. It had seemed to me that he had encouraged me to check more than my shirt, and it had crossed my mind that in our adult lives my brother and I had not seen each other naked.

Inside, I thought about that while I buttoned my shirt.

On the street, my brother opened my collar.

He smiled at me while he did it.

He touched my throat.

He undid another button.

He put his hand inside my shirt.

"Sweetheart," he said, "let's don't be uncomfy."

Along one of these mirrored walls, if pressed in the right spots, mirrored doors spring open. The clothes within, some from my brother's thinner years, vary in size. I am playing some Broadway scores while I try on my brother's clothes.

I play the records loud, too loud for this time of night, but I do not belt out songs. The young men across the street might hear me if I did.

I have not hummed "Moon River" yet.

The truth is that I have never loved this time of night, when the day that is over will not give up, or give in, or be left behind.

Soon the young men will be gone. It will not be long, either, I expect, before the lights on the mannequins will be turned off. I am assuming that the mannequins do not stay lighted through the day.

Though that, I suppose, is an assumption.

It was this time of the night, seven years ago, that I parted from my brother on the street. We did not part when we left the all-night bar. After that, there was nothing to do but go somewhere.

"Let's go to a *charming* bar," Nicholas said. "Let's discuss my life."

Nicholas wanted to go to a piano bar. He insisted it would be charming. He said we could get a drink in a glass.

As we walked, I saw my brother's face when we passed under streetlamps, and it struck me then that there is an event in the history of a face, after the extravagance of beauty has peaked and the pull of decline has just begun, when the beauty that is left to the face clings to the face in longing. It struck me that my brother had come to this event in the history of his beauty. For Nicholas, it was an event that could be called a transition.

Nicholas had an easy way of saying it.

"Have you noticed," he asked me as we walked, "that I am losing my face?"

I answered that everyone changes with age.

My brother said, "But I expected to be spared. I never thought that anything as dull as this would happen to me."

He laughed a little, at himself. He wanted, I think, to show me, with his laughter, that he realized he had been foolish in his notion. I was inclined to doubt that he realized this at all. It seemed to me likelier that he had laughed on the instinct that laughter was the called-for thing, the angling of the mask, but that in fact, he did not see anything unusual in having drifted through his life without it having crossed his mind, even once, that he would cease, one day, to be a creature whom others would cherish.

"This is my favorite place in the world," my brother said when we found a booth at the piano bar.

He asked what I had thought about the young man on the pool table.

I answered, because it was more or less true, that I had not had, about the young man on the pool table, anything that I would classify as a thought.

"I want to talk about pulchritude," my brother said. "What did you think of his pulchritude? I thought he had pulchritude. I thought he was toothsome in a sort of peaches-and-Budweiser kind of way. I mean, I thought he was comestible on what could be called a certain level."

I agreed that the young man on the pool table had been attractive on what could be called a level. I added that he had also been attractive in what could be called a fashion.

"Everything can be called a fashion," Nicholas said. "What do you think that kind of pulchritude gets for a night?"

I asked my brother to repeat what he had just said.

"*Mon-mon,*" Nicholas said. "How much do you think it costs? For a night?"

I gave my brother a look almost worthy, I thought, of looks he frequently gave me. Of course, he ignored it. Nicholas tended to ignore — or not to notice — looks he was not giving.

"Or do you think it's by the hour?" Nicholas asked. "I would want the night, I think."

I almost told my brother that it seemed to me that he would know this sort of thing better than I would. I almost told him to take the cost of the average netsuke and divide it by the toil of its acquisition. I did not say this. What I did say, because it was the truth, was that I had no idea.

"Neither do I," Nicholas said. "But it's time that I found out."

I asked why it was time.

"I am not going to lower my standards," Nicholas said. "With two people, it only works if one of them is stunning."

I said that it had been known to work when both were stunning.

"No," Nicholas said. "It does not really work between equals. I mean equal specimens. One person must be amazed to be with the other."

I suggested that it occasionally happens that both people are amazed.

Nicholas said, "There has to be gratitude in the act."

I told my brother that there often was.

"One person," my brother said, "must be *more* grateful."

I asked what made him think this.

My brother called me my name. It was one of the few times I could remember that Nicholas did not call me one of the endearments that he had for everyone.

When he spoke, he gave each word equal time.

"We are talking," he said, "about different things."

I said nothing. I knew we were.

"Now someone else," Nicholas said, "has got to be the stunning one."

In the piano bar, Nicholas drank beer from a bottle. He watched a woman stand behind the piano and sing a song that a famous singer had made her own. As he listened to the woman sing, my brother peeled the label from his bottle and stacked the shredded paper in the ashtray. When the woman held a note longer than required, Nicholas rolled his eyes.

"One can always depend," he said, "on the wrong people to have all the nerve. Some people should remember that there is a reason modesty is called a virtue."

When the woman finished, Nicholas did not applaud.

He went to the piano and spoke to the piano player. They had some discussion, and after it my brother wrapped his hand around the microphone. He made his fingers look long.

The piano player began the song, the one the woman had just finished singing, and Nicholas closed his eyes, made his face look rapt, raised his free hand to his face, touched his neck, his throat, arched his head back in the spotlight, and, starting slowly, released a long and quiet note.

My brother shaped the note into a word. The note

was round and open, then my brother took it to the end. He closed it, and with a gliding passage he rolled into the next. He kept his eyes closed and held himself straight in the dim spotlight through the first bars of the song. He could not have chosen better light for his face, or kinder light. He could not have wrapped his hand around the microphone with greater tenderness. On the microphone, my brother's fingers looked affectionate. Nicholas appeared to love the microphone, to love the song, each note that he was making, every sound that he produced, and even in his childhood, my brother could not have posed himself to look so like himself.

I may have been the last person in the bar to realize what Nicholas was doing with the song. He was not singing as himself. The voice that came out of him was not his. It was the voice of the famous singer who had made the song her own, her voice, her sound, that was coming from my brother. It came from within his body, from his chest, from his throat, and my brother shaped the singer's voice, without flaw, with his lips. In the purity of tone, in every stress laid on a lyric, in the tension of a note's duration and the snap with which the long-held note would break, Nicholas captured the singer's ways unerringly.

It was too perfect. If I had closed my eyes I would not have known that I was hearing imitation. Nicholas sang without the standard excess of impersonation. He did nothing more or less than sing exactly like the singer.

It was unplayful.

He could have overdone the singer's ways. He could have given the wink that makes impersonation safe. He had the chance to turn the song to parody, to give relief, and he did not give relief. When he came to the final note, the one that soars, he held it, held it some more, and then he let it fade as it fades in the recorded version of the song.

He had even taught himself to do that.

In my experience, in piano bars, when someone sings outstandingly, he is asked to sing again. But no one wanted more from Nicholas. There was no applause. I am sure he must have known that there would not be.

When he sat down, people were staring at him. Even though I knew that they were not, I felt that they were staring at us both.

I felt stared at.

I thought about the time, the practice, that Nicholas must have gone to, to teach himself to sing so exactly like the singer.

I asked him why he had not sung with his own voice, like himself.

Nicholas gave me a look that told me I had missed something.

"Why would I *sing* like myself?" my brother asked me. "I have never done anything like myself."

I wondered if Nicholas believed this.

I wondered if it was true.

Behind the mirrored doors, in the back of a drawer, under turtlenecks arranged by color, in envelopes marked by year, I find photographs of Nicholas, recent photographs, photographs that he did not blow up and frame as large as life.

I do not think that he would have called them shots.

Turtlenecks arranged by color, I gather, were my brother's filing system. What strikes me is that Nicholas had no need to keep these photographs and less need to hide them. No one but Nicholas lived here, no one was likely to look through his drawers, no one but the Spanish cleaning man who came twice a week, and I doubt that Nicholas would have worried about a cleaning man sneering over unbecoming photographs.

I spread them on the cashmere blanket to compare the best and worst. The difference is not between one and another. The difference is between these hidden photographs and the figure in the Japanese robe.

The difference is between the hidden photographs and Nicholas.

What I am wondering is why he kept these photographs, why he hid them, and why he hid them where he did, in a place where they could so easily be taken out and looked at. If they had been mine, I would have put them at the bottom of a chest, a deep chest packed inside with things impossible to move. If I were going to take the pains to hide a thing from sight, I would take the pains to make it hard to see.

More likely, I would have thrown them away.

I am wondering why Nicholas did not. I am wondering if now and then he took them out from under the turtlenecks to look at them, to study them, perhaps, and if he did, how often, and why, and what, I wonder, did he think when he studied them.

There is no ball-point on these photographs.

No blue hollows carved into the cheeks.

And when the young men came into this room, the young men my brother paid, when they saw the blown-up, life-size photograph from years ago, the photograph in the mirrored frame of the creature in the Japanese robe, how, I am wondering, did Nicholas answer the question, which one young man or other must have asked — the question of who the figure in the Japanese robe, in the mirrored frame, was.

Who it had been.

I am wondering if my brother smiled, laughed, gave the young man a remnant of a look, pointed to the photograph, then at himself, and asked the young man why he thought he was being paid.

That is what I would like to think my brother did.

When my brother told me that he was paying young men — when he called me a few nights after the night in the piano bar to tell me that he had paid a man for the first time — I told him there were limits.

I believed there were.

Even so, I found myself wondering that night seven years ago if he had waited until he was alone to call me, or if he was calling me from his bed, with the man still in it.

I asked him why he could not find someone to be equal with.

My brother made a sound into the telephone. The sound he made was not a word.

I told my brother that most people chose to be with peers. I asked why he did not.

"*What* peers?" Nicholas asked.

In the lacquer now I see my brother framed in red. I find his eyes in places where the red layers have worn away by nature, or, if I am wrong about the table, where the black base has been forced through by the industry of monks. I am hoping to learn that this table is the real item. Presents to Nicholas should have been authentic. My brother's eyes, in life, were no less black than this.

The skull faces behind him, the ones along the wall of the ball court, compete in the red lacquer with my brother's face, and it is my brother's face prevailing.

Behind one of the mirrored doors, I find my brother's robes. He had a collection, quite a number. Some, I think, are based on old designs; some, I think, are old. Reaching in, I touch the hanging silk and wonder which robe might be the one that my brother had on last.

I find myself wondering if Nicholas liked conversations with the young men, in intervals, if there were intervals, and if he gave a young man a robe to put on while they spoke.

I am wondering if the last young man wore one of these robes.

If he did, I find myself wondering why he, the last young man, did not take it. I find myself wondering why he did not take my brother's netsukes, why not everything in malachite.

The man in Chichén Itzá's diamond cuff links are still here, and there is money in my brother's trousers on the floor.

Too much is here, and I find myself asking the last young man why he did not take things, why he did not smash the tequila bottle on the table and scratch broken glass across the lacquer, just to kill my brother thoroughly.

That is what I find myself wondering as I compare my brother's robes.

Of all of them, the one in the photograph is, without a doubt, the one. It is the best. There is a landscape in the lining; crimson trees pierce embroidered sky; animals play in the river. The silk against my skin is a feeling Nicholas would have had a word for.

The robe almost fits, which seems wrong; Nicholas was always so much smaller. Yet the obi goes around me. Not twice, it is true, but it goes around.

In my brother's robe, I lean against the picture glass, against the skulls in Chichén Itzá.

When we were there together, before we climbed the pyramid, before he met the man in the open madras shirt who wore French cuffs to dinner, Nicholas read aloud to me one night in bed. He read that when Chichén Itzá was a city and the ball court was in use for sport, the players played sometimes for gold, sometimes for the right to strip the spectators of their clothes. He read a description of the ball that had figured in the game, of how that ball was made. He read to me that holes had been drilled into trees to disgorge a sap, great white drops of it, which then would harden and be molded and turn black.

It took us time to realize that all that he was reading about was the making of rubber, and when we realized this together, we laughed at the same time.

Nicholas was still laughing when he read to me that it was the winner of the match, that it was not the loser, who gave up his life in sacrifice, and that men trained hard to win the honor.

I do not know if Nicholas remembered what he read to me in laughter, or if he knew, through all the years that he could see himself posed against it, framed in mirrors in this room, that the wall of skulls behind him was where the winners' heads were laid.

VINTAGE
CONTEMPORARIES

___ **Love Always** by Ann Beattie	$5.95	394-74418-7
___ **First Love and Other Sorrows** by Harold Brodkey	$5.95	679-72075-8
___ **The Debut** by Anita Brookner	$5.95	394-72856-4
___ **Cathedral** by Raymond Carver	$4.95	394-71281-1
___ **Bop** by Maxine Chernoff	$5.95	394-75522-7
___ **I Look Divine** by Christopher Coe	$5.95	394-75995-8
___ **Dancing Bear** by James Crumley	$5.95	394-72576-X
___ **The Last Good Kiss** by James Crumley	$6.95	394-75989-3
___ **One to Count Cadence** by James Crumley	$5.95	394-73559-5
___ **The Wrong Case** by James Crumley	$5.95	394-73558-7
___ **The Last Election** by Pete Davies	$6.95	394-74702-X
___ **A Narrow Time** by Michael Downing	$6.95	394-75568-5
___ **From Rockaway** by Jill Eisenstadt	$6.95	394-75761-0
___ **Platitudes** by Trey Ellis	$6.95	394-75439-5
___ **Days Between Stations** by Steve Erickson	$6.95	394-74685-6
___ **Rubicon Beach** by Steve Erickson	$6.95	394-75513-8
___ **A Fan's Notes** by Frederick Exley	$7.95	679-72076-6
___ **Pages from a Cold Island** by Frederick Exley	$6.95	394-75977-X
___ **A Piece of My Heart** by Richard Ford	$5.95	394-72914-5
___ **Rock Springs** by Richard Ford	$6.95	394-75700-9
___ **The Sportswriter** by Richard Ford	$6.95	394-74325-3
___ **The Ultimate Good Luck** by Richard Ford	$5.95	394-75089-6
___ **Fat City** by Leonard Gardner	$5.95	394-74316-4
___ **Ellen Foster** by Kaye Gibbons	$5.95	394-75757-2
___ **Within Normal Limits** by Todd Grimson	$5.95	394-74617-1
___ **Airships** by Barry Hannah	$5.95	394-72913-7
___ **Dancing in the Dark** by Janet Hobhouse	$5.95	394-72588-3
___ **November** by Janet Hobhouse	$6.95	394-74665-1
___ **Saigon, Illinois** by Paul Hoover	$6.95	394-75849-8
___ **Fiskadoro** by Denis Johnson	$5.95	394-74367-9
___ **The Stars at Noon** by Denis Johnson	$5.95	394-75427-1
___ **Asa, as I Knew Him** by Susanna Kaysen	$4.95	394-74985-5
___ **Lulu Incognito** by Raymond Kennedy	$6.95	394-75641-X
___ **Steps** by Jerzy Kosinski	$5.95	394-75716-5
___ **A Handbook for Visitors From Outer Space** by Kathryn Kramer	$5.95	394-72989-7
___ **The Chosen Place, the Timeless People** by Paule Marshall	$6.95	394-72633-2
___ **Suttree** by Cormac McCarthy	$6.95	394-74145-5
___ **The Bushwhacked Piano** by Thomas McGuane	$5.95	394-72642-1
___ **Nobody's Angel** by Thomas McGuane	$6.95	394-74738-0
___ **Something to Be Desired** by Thomas McGuane	$4.95	394-73156-5
___ **To Skin a Cat** by Thomas McGuane	$5.95	394-75521-9
___ **Bright Lights, Big City** by Jay McInerney	$5.95	394-72641-3
___ **Ransom** by Jay McInerney	$5.95	394-74118-8
___ **The All-Girl Football Team** by Lewis Nordan	$5.95	394-75701-7
___ **River Dogs** by Robert Olmstead	$6.95	394-74684-8

VINTAGE
CONTEMPORARIES

___ **Soft Water** by Robert Olmstead	$6.95	394-75752-1
___ **Family Resemblances** by Lowry Pei	$6.95	394-75528-6
___ **Norwood** by Charles Portis	$5.95	394-72931-5
___ **Clea & Zeus Divorce** by Emily Prager	$6.95	394-75591-X
___ **A Visit From the Footbinder** by Emily Prager	$6.95	394-75592-8
___ **Mohawk** by Richard Russo	$6.95	394-74409-8
___ **Anywhere But Here** by Mona Simpson	$6.95	394-75559-6
___ **Carnival for the Gods** by Gladys Swan	$6.95	394-74330-X
___ **Myra Breckinridge and Myron** by Gore Vidal	$8.95	394-75444-1
___ **The Car Thief** by Theodore Weesner	$6.95	394-74097-1
___ **Breaking and Entering** by Joy Williams	$6.95	394-75773-4
___ **Taking Care** by Joy Williams	$5.95	394-72912-9

On sale at bookstores everywhere, but if otherwise unavailable, may be ordered from us. You can use this coupon, or phone (800) 638-6460.

Please send me the Vintage Contemporaries books I have checked on the reverse. I am enclosing
$ _____ (add $1.00 per copy to cover postage and handling). Send
check or money order—no cash or CODs, please. Prices are subject to change without notice.

NAME _____

ADDRESS _____

CITY _____ STATE _____ ZIP _____

Send coupons to:
RANDOM HOUSE, INC., 400 Hahn Road, Westminster, MD 21157
ATTN: ORDER ENTRY DEPARTMENT
Allow at least 4 weeks for delivery.

005   38